Rana Haddad grew up in Lattakia in Syria, moved to the UK as a teenager, and read English Literature at Cambridge University. She has since worked as a journalist for the BBC, Channel 4, and other broadcasters, and has also published poetry. *The Unexpected Love Objects of Dunya Noor* is her first novel.

The Unexpected Love Objects of Dunya Noor

Rana Haddad

hoopoe

AN IMPRINT OF AUC PRESS

First published in 2018 by
Hoopoe
113 Sharia Kasr el Aini, Cairo, Egypt
420 Fifth Avenue, New York, 10018
www.hoopoefiction.com

Hoopoe is an imprint of the American University in Cairo Press
www.aucpress.com

Exclusive distribution outside Egypt and North America by I.B.Tauris & Co Ltd., 6
Salem Road, London, W2 4BU

Dar el Kutub No. 11310/17
ISBN 978 977 416 861 1

Dar el Kutub Cataloging-in-Publication Data

Haddad, Rana
        The Unexpected Love Objects of Dunya Noor / Rana Haddad.—Cairo:
    The American University in Cairo Press, 2018.
        p.   cm.
        ISBN: 978 977 416 861 1
        1. English fiction
        832

1 2 3 4 5   22 21 20 19 18

Designed by Adam el-Sehemy
Printed in the United States of America

The events of this book take place during the fin de siècle period of the last century, when a mustachioed military dictator, with an abnormally large head, named Hafez al-Assad (father of Bashar) ruled Syria.

Prologue

Dunya Noor had once heard that, when love occurred, the object of her love would begin to sparkle, because true love often appeared in the unexpected form of *light*. Was this really true? Only God knew—only God and possibly also her camera. All she would need to do was to take a photograph of that light if and when it shone in the face of her beloved, that was how she'd prove that he was the One.

For there could only ever be One.

There could only ever be One God, One Father, One Mother, only One.

There could only ever be One Sun in the sky, One Moon, only One.

And in a country like Syria, there could only ever be One Truth, only One, and there was only one man who knew it— and his name was Hafez al-Assad.

BOOK ONE
An English Rose

1

The Beauty Contest

IT WAS THE SUMMER OF 1996 in the Democratic Arab Republic of Syria and the sun was blazing above its most important, but little known, Mediterranean harbor city of Latakia. On the large and marble-tiled terrace of the old colonial Casino Hotel, five young women stood on an elevated platform, each next to her own specially designated bamboo chair. They flicked their hair, stood up, walked about, and allowed the audience to judge them.

Dr. Joseph Noor carefully inspected the girls and tried to make up his mind as to who should win. He glanced at the audience behind him: a collection of heavily made-up and overly perfumed society women and their pampered, pot-bellied husbands. He tried to avoid looking at his English wife Patricia, because he suspected that she was about to cry, as she sometimes did during such occasions. He could hear her heavy breathing next to him and feel her agitated movements. Out of the corner of his eye, Dr. Joseph Noor saw his wife crossing one of her legs over the other and then uncrossing it, over and over again, and instead of looking at him or at any of the contestants, she distracted herself either by inspecting her expensive designer shoes or by sipping loudly from a glass of bitter lemon which she put back on the table next to her with a sharp bang. It was as if Patricia was trying to force Joseph to take notice of her. But Joseph continued to ignore her and instead stared at the beautiful young contestants, assessing each one according to her merits.

Attending Latakia's annual beauty contest was becoming more and more difficult for Patricia as the years went by, because (according to her self-critical green eyes and the large bedroom mirror custom-made for her in a famous glass factory in Damascus), her own once-striking beauty was now fading.

"I think Dunya would've won if she'd been here," Patricia whispered in her husband's ear. Her long artificial eyelashes swayed a little, like lost exclamation marks.

"I disagree," Joseph said gruffly, while observing a contestant who wore a sophisticated blue hat, "I think Jamila Zamani is far prettier."

Patricia looked at Jamila contemptuously and said, "Huh?" She saw Joseph's rude comment as a snub to herself as well as to their daughter Dunya, who had always managed to get on her father's nerves, even though she lived at a distance of at least four thousand kilometers in a northwesterly direction (England).

"You have the strangest taste in women, Joseph," Patricia said.

"Perhaps that's why I married you," Joseph answered.

"She's our only child. Why do you dislike her so much?" Patricia looked at Joseph.

"She's not a child any more, Patricia. She's a strange young woman who prefers her camera to a decent man. What kind of daughter is that? No family in Syria has ever had a daughter like ours." Joseph huffed and puffed until his yellow short-sleeved shirt started to shake visibly, and he didn't stop huffing until his straw hat fell on the floor and rolled away like an irresponsible thought.

"But Hilal is a decent man, isn't he? And she loves him, more than her camera, I should think," Patricia said.

"*Hilal!* Please don't mention that name in front of me. How can I allow my daughter to marry a man whose name is Hilal? And besides, how can you call someone whose job it is to stare at the moon a man?" Joseph's face puffed up

4

like some strange pastry—he looked like a balloon that was about to explode.

"He's an astronomer, Joseph. It's his job to study the moon and contemplate the stars. Just because no one practices astronomy in Syria doesn't make it a disreputable profession," Patricia said. "Dunya says he's about to discover a theory! He's probably a genius—what more could you want from a son-in-law?"

"He is a Muslim, remember? Do you want our daughter married to a Muslim?"

"I don't care if he's a Muslim as long as she loves him. And besides, he's handsome, so very, very handsome."

"You're English and that is why you'll never understand," Joseph said. He turned away from Patricia and concentrated his gaze at Jamila Zamani, his favorite contestant. Her hat had just been plucked by a grasping sea bird and she'd caught her dress in the back of her bamboo chair. Joseph gasped in embarrassment, but he wished that his own daughter was a little bit more like Jamila: engaged to an architect from a good Greek Orthodox Christian family, and had recently graduated (with flying colors) in law.

"She'd be an idiot to marry a man like that Hilal, the son of a *tailor.*"

"What is wrong with tailors? I love tailors. Yves St. Laurent is a tailor, isn't he?"

If he'd had a gun, Joseph would have liked to be able to use it right then, to pull the trigger and shoot that man who was plotting to steal his daughter.

But luckily Hilal was out of reach, munching a biscuit on an airplane that was bulleting its way toward Damascus airport as fast as it could.

As Mr. and Mrs. Noor were twirling their thumbs waiting for the beauty contest results, and after Joseph had cast his vote, his best friend Salman Ghazi came toward them, beaming.

Mr. Ghazi was an exceptionally loudmouthed lawyer who normally described himself as an 'avocado'—an Arabization of the French word 'avocat,' which means lawyer.

"Patricia tells me that Dunya's coming home next week, is that true?" Mr. Ghazi asked Joseph. "Why didn't you tell us? Maria will be over the moon when she hears of this."

"She only told us of her visit this morning."

"She flies out of the country in the dead of night without saying goodbye and then turns up all of a sudden, *ten years later*, without warning? I thought you preferred to visit her in England. What if . . . ?" Mr. Ghazi cut his own nervous whisper short.

"What if *what*?" Joseph asked.

"What if she gets herself into trouble again?" Mr. Ghazi said.

"She's no longer the reckless little girl she used to be. She's a grown-up woman now, with her head on her shoulders." Joseph said this with some hesitation. "Patricia and I are getting tired of flying so often to see her and she's missing Syria. It's time she came back."

"If it's true she's a reformed character as you say, perhaps you should find her a husband while she's here, Joseph. Isn't she Maria's age? Don't leave it too late. And remember, I can help you find the right husband for her. You don't want her to marry a cold fish of an Englishman, do you?"

"It's too early for her to be thinking about husbands, she needs to concentrate on her studies and her career first. I don't want her to be a wife right now, Salman, she's not ready for it. Our girls are not like their mothers, they need to be independent and then find a husband later."

"I expect she'll become a doctor won't she?" Salman said.

"She wants to be a photographer."

"A photographer? You must be joking. Don't you want her to be a heart surgeon like you, or at least a dentist, or a, or a . . ."

"She's made up her mind, Salman."

"Well, how about a lawyer, a banker? Who wants his daughter to be a photographer? What's she going to photograph? Who's going to pay her to take photographs?"

"Well, photography seems to be a good career in England. Apparently it's considered an art," Joseph said with a clear lack of conviction.

"Don't believe what she tells you. Only an Armenian would think photography is a career, that and hairdressing. Even my wife, who is good at nothing but complaining, can take good photographs. It's not a skill. I'll talk her out of it— if you can't. When a girl is wilful it's an art to lead her to the right path. They always say boys are difficult, but in my opinion girls are more so and their lack of obedience more dangerous. You need to learn from me, Joseph, look at my daughter Maria. She does what I say."

A big copper bell rang and some ecstatic belly dance music blared out of the five loud speakers. "The winner of this year's Miss Latakia Beauty Contest is Maria Ghazi. Hey, Maria, come onto the stage," boomed a rather macho voice. And the beauty queen was duly crowned to the applause of the crowd and awarded twenty pairs of Yves St. Laurent shoes (a year's supply) as well as a five-star holiday for two in Greece.

A whole balcony full of Latakians clapped bitterly because their daughters hadn't won. They muttered to one another, "Anyway, who cares! What kind of cheap prize is this? And if Maria goes to Greece with one of her friends they'll certainly get up to no good and no one will *ever* want to marry them when they come back. What a loose generation this is!"

Mr. Ghazi looked at his daughter Maria proudly. "Oh darling, I knew you'd win. Your granny will take you to Greece, and you'll have a whale of a time there." He burst into a bombastic belly laugh, which caused his mustache to jump up and down. Maria looked disturbed by what she'd heard but she kept her mouth shut. Mr. Ghazi had decided that she would go to Greece in the company of her half-blind granny Anaïs, who hadn't had a trip abroad for the last forty years. And what Mr. Ghazi decided was always law. Who would dare cross him?

Granny Anaïs had been far too busy breaking news hither and thither to have had time to travel. She was the Central City Gossip, a prominent member of Latakia's daily morning gossip clubs, which operated as an environmentally friendly alternative to newspapers. Instead of wasting precious paper, they only needed air to circulate. Their mainly female members worked as unpaid information hubs; they were Latakia's very own news agencies. And being half blind she was able to see the strangest things; her tongue wagged constantly in anticipation of terrible scandals and disaster.

Maria suddenly wished that she hadn't won the competition. There was no way she could go to Greece with her fiancé Shadi because that would be considered indecent by every decent person in the city, but going in the company of her grandmother Anaïs would bring her to her knees.

Joseph stood up and stared at the horizon with sad and worried eyes. The Mediterranean Sea spread in front of him for miles, blue and magnificent and indifferent to his petty family squabbles. He felt faint and he wondered whether it would happen to him one day, "Am I really going to die of a heart attack and will it be because of Dunya or Patricia, or a fatal combination of the two?"

2

Mr. and Mrs. Noor

EVERYONE KNEW THAT JOSEPH NOOR was the most famous heart surgeon in the Syrian Arab Republic. He was famous for having rescued most of the high and mighty in the country from possible death by heart dysfunction or heart attack. To be attacked by one's heart was quite a common occurrence in Syria, particularly for men. The problem with Joseph Noor was that his heart also had a will of its own, and had launched a few attacks on him at regular intervals since the age of six when he'd heard that, like his father Ibrahim, he might one day become bald. It was rare for a child of only six to fall down for such reasons. As a result, his mother Marrouma began to see him as an extremely sensitive and fragile boy and began to spoil him rotten. And all of his family made sure that Joseph Noor grew up to be one of the most spoiled men in the city, perhaps in the country, possibly in the whole wide world. Spoiling him to death seemed like the only way to save Joseph's life.

Thus it came about that his heart was the center of his life and Joseph became obsessed not merely with the medical aspects of hearts in general, but his own in particular. He thought that if he learned all about the human heart he might be able to save his own from itself indefinitely.

Apart from its propensity to launch attacks at him, Joseph's heart seemed to lack other interests. He had never fallen in love or been passionate about any woman or felt any particularly tender feelings toward anyone until he reached the ripe age of twenty-eight.

At his birthday party, which took place in a pub in London near Imperial College, where as an undergraduate he was slowly plotting to take over world heart surgery, Joseph glimpsed a girl sitting on a chair. The moment he saw her, Joseph stopped being able to see anything else at all in the room, and walked straight toward her. He stood in front of her, red as a rose and smiling like the village idiot.

The girl had never met a man with such curly black hair in her life before, nor such a big nose. She didn't understand why he was smiling as he was and not saying a word. Suddenly a sentence made its way out of his mouth in a sort of whisper, "What is your name?"

She thought he was trying to flirt with her—which he was—but instead of responding with an encouraging smile, she gave him a hard slap on the face and briskly walked out. One reason for her cruelty was that all of Joseph's doctor friends were looking on from behind them and laughing. She thought he'd made a bet with them and was about to make a fool of her.

As she walked out into the fresh air, she found Joseph following her. His hair was on end and he had a pleading look in his eyes. "I really need to know your name."

"Pat-ricia," she said.

"Patri-cia?" He looked at her for a moment as if he were looking at someone or something that it had never occurred to him he might come across. "I've never heard of such a beautiful name before," he said in a gentle voice.

Joseph became perfectly quiet and didn't know what else to say. She was, he thought, the most beautiful woman he had ever set his eyes upon. Her green eyes and her tall majestic figure, her blond hair and her elegant aristocratic cheekbones, everything about her was perfect, including her subtle air of cold haughtiness which made his heart beat ten times faster than it should. She had that sort of icy beauty that not many women in Syria had and which he found irresistible.

Patricia could tell from his accent that Joseph was a foreigner. She thought he might be French, Jewish, or Spanish—at any rate, someone who clearly belonged to a culture marked by curly hair and random emotional outbursts.

He had correctly calculated that Patricia might find his pretended ignorance endearing. "I've never heard of such a beautiful name before." This was the only sentence he had ever invented for the delicate purpose of ensnaring a woman, and as if by miracle, it worked.

The two married within six months of meeting and Joseph promised Patricia that they would live in London and that he would become famous. But after only four years of living in a rented apartment in Marylebone, while Joseph effortlessly climbed the ladder of success in the heart surgery world, he woke up one morning and said to her, "I cannot bear this any longer."

"You can't bear what?"

"I cannot bear London. I feel it's suffocating me."

"Well, we could move to the country, darling. I could teach you golf. You'd love it."

"No, Patricia. I need to live in Latakia."

"Latakia? What do you mean, Latakia? What about me? How am I supposed to live there? You wait until I'm pregnant to tell me this? What about the baby? Do you want your children to grow up in *Latakia*?"

"Well, why not? I grew up there and look at me, as good as gold, as sound as a bell!"

Latakia was nothing special to the unaddicted eye. If you did not happen to be born there it might never have any sort of hold on you. It never succeeded in getting a hold on Patricia who found it boring, parochial, and cement-ridden.

"Joseph, why do you keep on calling it a *she*?" Patricia soon started to get irritated. "It's just an ugly little town."

Since they moved back he'd been frantically showing Latakia off to her.

"You act as if we're in Venice," Patricia often said resentfully.

"You say that because you're a snob. You think the only worthwhile place on earth is England. You English are so cold, your judgments can't be trusted."

Latakia had many problems as a town: it was full of unpainted buildings with television aerials sticking out of them like unkempt hair, its streets were half-finished, and its trees were painted white up to the top of their trunks, to deter cockroaches from traveling up and devouring the leaves and likely fruits of the season.

Despite its many glaring defects Latakia seemed to exert a strange influence on its inhabitants, most of whom developed feelings for it that could only be described as romantic. Most dyed-in-the-wool Latakians often thought of their city as a beautiful girl. Her official moniker was 'Bride of the Sea.'

Patricia thought that this might be a psychological condition, brought on by a mixture of heat and totalitarianism, as Syria was a superstar police state, and Latakia—which was the apple of President Hafez al-Assad's eye—because he was born in a village nearby—had fast become a satellite beach resort of neo-Stalinism. It had an array of Russian ships regularly patrolling its harbor and pictures of the heart-throb president pasted on every surface imaginable, from car windows to school classrooms. In one such picture, his head replaced a pearl inside an open shell; he smiled beatifically. Everybody's heart had to beat for one person: Mr. al-Assad. Everyone insisted that they were ready to sacrifice their lives for his beautiful eyes or for his alluring mustache.

Anything less than that was considered political treason.

Joseph couldn't understand why Patricia didn't fall for Syria's charms, or why she was constantly pining for the abnormally green grass of England, because like most Syrians he believed that his country was the best country on earth, that they had the best trees, the best food, the best mountains, and the best sea.

Latakia seemed to generate a syndrome in some of its inhabitants generally known as Superiority Syndrome, and otherwise known as a Superiority Complex. Not only, as general opinion had it, did ancient Latakians (in nearby Ugarit) invent and give birth to the alphabet as we know it (A, B, C, D) but the genius Arabs had also given the world algebra, and the mystical non-number zero—as well as three world religions. They had given the world God himself.

Latakia was born lucky, at least four thousand years ago, and had survived seven earthquakes in the interim, as well as many natural, social, and political disasters—so people assumed it was an immortal city. They also assumed that whatever disasters might befall her at present, she would inevitably rise again like the phoenix and take the world by storm. Superiority Syndrome reigned supreme.

Patricia never understood all of this and never forgave Syrians, and particularly Latakians, for being so pleased with their past achievements that they ignored their present failings to a point that, in any European city, would be regarded as criminal neglect.

But despite her barely hidden scorn and because of her striking looks and blond hair, Patricia became an instant hit in Latakia and was treated like visiting royalty from the moment she set foot in the city; all of Joseph's friends were green with envy.

Although she enjoyed the attention at first, Patricia soon fell into a deep state of depression, because, apart from socializing and gossiping, there was nothing for a woman of her social status to do. Even going shopping was considered too low class for her and could cause a major scandal, which would destroy Joseph Noor and his entire family's carefully guarded reputation in a matter of seconds.

Moments after her mother-in-law Marrouma saw Patricia going into a butcher's shop one morning wearing a slightly flimsy summer dress, Joseph received a hysterical phone call. "How can you let *your wife* go and mix with all the lowlifes? Why is she shopping in the first place? Can't Dr. Joseph Noor send a boy to buy his wife's groceries for her? And if you saw what she was wearing your heart would've exploded! She even smiled at the butcher and chatted with him as if he were her long-lost friend. What will people say, Joseph?"

It only took Patricia a few months of residence in Latakia to grow to reciprocate her mother-in-law's open hostility. From Marrouma's point of view, Patricia was "Not From Here," and she didn't deserve the most handsome young man in Syria. A man not just intellectual and kind, but who also possessed blue eyes. "Where she comes from, most men have blue eyes and she could have had her pick," she often said. Marrouma regarded Patricia as a cunning son-thief skilfully disguised as an elegant and beautiful woman, who was as foreign as the French but, in fact, English. Altogether she must be a thief, because it was a commonly acknowledged fact that "all the colonials did was to rob our country dry"—even when it came to husbands.

Despite the relentless negative publicity campaign orchestrated against Patricia by her mother-in-law, almost everyone in Latakia fell head over heels for her. She became an instant celebrity; their token blonde woman, their local fashion icon, and a reminder of the outside world, which most people had never been to but had watched with fascination and awe on cinema and television screens.

Poor Marrouma swiftly turned into an archetypally evil mother-in-law, while Patricia's popularity only served to fan the flames of her hatred.

3

Mustache Power

DUNYA'S CURLY HAIR, WHICH SHE inherited from her father Joseph, flew up in small circles, defying the laws of fashion and gravity. This was not a good look to have for a girl in Latakia.

And, as if to make things worse, Dunya was also born with what was generally considered a big mouth—also regarded as a major handicap for a girl in Latakia. Instead of learning how to say the right thing at the right time, she seemed to relish saying the very opposite of what was expected.

She had another strange quality, which in Latakia was considered unbecoming and even dangerous for a girl: curiosity. She liked to look at things—almost anything—as if she thought that the more she looked at it, the more an object or a person would reveal their mystery to her. She appeared to see mysteries in things that were commonly believed to have none. On the whole, it was agreed that it was as if she were not really the daughter of Mr. and Mrs. Noor. She was neither sufficiently Patricia-like nor Joseph-like, nor a gratifying combination of the two.

Granny Marrouma, who was increasingly exasperated at Joseph's continued adulation of his wife and his refusal to publicly acknowledge that he had made a mistake in marrying an English woman, revenged herself against him by also persecuting Dunya—whenever the opportunity presented itself.

"It's a pity you didn't get your mother's blond hair, although it does make her look a little unintelligent. Still, it

15

helped her catch a husband, didn't it?" Marrouma would mutter while Dunya sat on her lap. Then she would play with Dunya's hair as if it were a weird shrub and say plaintively, "Such curls don't suit girls. I wonder who will ever marry you when you grow up. And, what's more, you're neither this nor that, you're a *mongrel*!"

Patricia would try to protect her daughter. "Madame Marrouma, stop talking to her about husbands, she's too young for that."

"I'm only telling the truth," Marrouma would insist.

Things only got worse when it was time for Dunya to go to school.

When Patricia saw the sort of uniforms that girls were required to wear, she almost fainted. Even in the most exclusive school, the School of the Carmelite Nuns where she was expected to send her daughter, military khakis with black boots and black socks were de rigueur (after the age of eleven). Wearing even brown or dark blue socks was against school regulation and punishable by caning. Wearing yellow or red socks was considered a sign of open mutiny and could lead to serious disciplinary action. Short nails were compulsory and no jewelery allowed, apart from the plainest earrings, which were to be affixed to some girls' ears within hours of their birth (as a mark of their gender), and always in the color blue, which it was rumored had the power to avert the dangerous influence of the evil eye—a curse mechanism believed to be widespread in Syria and caused by excessive envy.

When Patricia heard that her soon to be Syrian-educated daughter would be trained to use a machine gun as part of her future education, all her fears about living away from England were confirmed. "Joseph, I told you this is not a place for our daughter to grow up!"

Joseph thought his wife was being racist and that she was overreacting to what in fact was nothing more than a show. He believed that this sort of show of patriotism was important in a country that was, technically speaking, at war. Once peace was established, all this totalitarian nonsense and playing with guns would be abandoned; Joseph was willing to be patient.

Since the late forties, Syria had been at daggers drawn with one of its newly created neighbors, Israel, a country that had not existed since biblical times and whose traumatic rebirth had caused all hell to break loose. The Syrian army kept sending them their tanks, which always came back battered, but always claiming victory. What kind of victory it was, no one dared to ask.

"It's your fault anyway. You British," Joseph often told his wife. "You gave it to them and it wasn't yours to give!"

"Yes, darling. Everything is always our fault. We are always apologizing, darling. We are always so very sorry."

Joseph wished that he hadn't fallen in love with an offspring of the colonials, but he couldn't help it. And now it was too late. Marriage, he mused, was an eternal knot. Patricia became increasingly unhappy at living in what she saw not only as one of the least known cities on Earth, but also possibly the ugliest one! She was unable to accept her fate as a citizen of Latakia and considered herself a reluctant visitor who was always about to leave. But despite her regular attempts, Patricia miserably failed to convince her husband that it was time for them to abandon his patriotic experiment and move back to England. So she spent most of her spare time crying and crying. Sometimes Patricia contemplated running away, though she was afraid that if she took that route (which would involve kidnapping Dunya as in Syrian law the father always keeps the children), she might inadvertently kill Joseph—because of his volatile heart. Joseph's illness gave him the power of veto: it was, as ever, the ace up his sleeve.

At other times Patricia tried to use Joseph's heart as an excuse for immigrating back to England, where the health care was vastly superior. "You can't operate on yourself, can you? Who can you trust in Latakia to operate on you? Are you telling me you're prepared to die for love of your country?" But Joseph was stubborn as a goat, and his answer was always, "Yes, I am."

When Patricia finally understood that she would have to spend the rest of her life in Syria, she went to the hairdresser Shahira and asked to have her hair dyed black. This was not only a public display of depression at discovering the truth of her dark fate; she also did it because she had become sick of being stared at. Her blondeness had turned her into a local sex symbol; a status that was inappropriate for the mother of a young child, she thought. She also did it to upset Joseph, of course.

The hairdresser, who loved Patricia's hair and felt lucky to be honored with the task of trimming it, shed a tear while she was applying the chemical dye and refused to take payment.

"You're not the woman I married," Joseph said. "You look like everyone else's wives now." Patricia's physical transformation came to him like a stab: sharp, deadly, and straight where it hurt (his ego).

That was when Patricia started her long vigil of mourning for her own life. (Although her black hair did not last for more than a season.)

What Patricia had failed to appreciate was that Syria was in the throes of a rather interesting revolutionary experiment: a Dictatorship of the Proletariat. It was something that sounded so novel at the time that most well-meaning people didn't immediately run a mile. On the contrary, it actually motivated some men, like Joseph, to return home instead of living abroad. The man who had started it all was Mr. Hafez al-Assad (whose name happened to mean the 'Protector Lion') and he had called it 'Demoqratiya al-Shaabiya,' meaning 'Democracy of the People.' Patricia was not unimpressed by Hafez al-Assad to start with. Women loved him because he was considered good looking (the usual) and men admired him because he used to be a pilot and because it was rumored that he cried when he was forced to kill one of his two rivals during the ascent to power. Three men had undertaken to rule the land. That was clearly impossible. Assad promised a golden age but instead he promptly turned his own country into a cage. A huge number of people were sent to jail either for thinking, saying, or doing the 'wrong' thing. He took most of the land and the factories from a handful of Sunni and Greek Orthodox men and redistributed them to the people. This happened on March 8, 1970.

As the number eight in Arabic looks like a Syrian mustache:

∧

Ever since that day, having a mustache of that sort was considered a patriotic gesture.

Joseph came back to Syria because he wanted to see his country progress and to give a helping hand. Why not? What is patriotism for, if not for men with mustaches to help one another? Joseph didn't dare to grow any type of mustache, however, because Patricia forbade him to.

A Syrian mustache was one of the highest male expressions of patriotism, a gesture where both mind and body were united.

The men in mustaches did a lot of good. First of all they changed the law and gave women greater equality with men (in theory, at least, more than that would be indecent). There was a mushrooming of free education for all and free hospitals (where rats could run freely). The countryside was to be electrically empowered and water, water everywhere, though (often) not a drop to drink. And this was all thanks to the Euphrates Dam project, which made damn sure that Syria's biggest river was turned into a god again—becoming the source of most electrical enlightenment.

The reason that the Democracy of the People traumatized Patricia so much was because it was nothing more than a euphemism, and soon the dreams of the masses turned into a nightmare as bad and grim as what had transpired before them; as bad and grim as the four hundred years of Ottoman rule by bamboo stick and feudal rule by the boot, followed by colonialism, when Syria was flooded with French nuns and priests, who prayed loudly and preached, while French colonels stole all the tobacco that grew on Syria's shores and shipped it to Paris. The French had found it hard to leave Syria because they loved hummus far too much and got a taste for a dish called kibbeh, as well as kebab, but the Syrians convinced them to leave in the end using a world-renowned, much-tested traditional method: the barrel of the gun.

After hordes of Phoenicians, Babylonians, Assyrians, Caledonians, Romans, Byzantines, Muhammedans, Ottomans, the feudal lords, and the French, Hafez al-Assad's Baath Party and its band of mustachioed young men decided that it was time for them to rule Syria. And it was then that the rule by mustache officially began.

Since then only a man with a mustache born in the vicinity of Kurdaha (a tiny Alawite village near Latakia) was allowed to have any sort of political power. Hafez al-Assad was born in Kurdaha and because his brothers and cousins were also born there, many of the uncouth and streetwise toughs of Kurdaha swiftly rose to the highest echelons of government and ruled Syria Mafia-style.

The barrel of the gun was still as popular as ever.

4

First Love

WHEN DUNYA FELL IN LOVE for the first time, the object of her undying love and affection raised many eyebrows. It had never been heard of before nor considered possible that an eight-year-old girl could fall in love with a camera. It just wasn't normal. She'd been absent-mindedly walking with her mother when she glimpsed the window display of the only photography shop in Latakia, Studio Maurice. Dunya froze where she stood, forcing the bewildered Patricia to stop, too. She looked at the black metallic machines that lay demurely there—wasting away—and settled her gaze on an antique-looking Kodak camera.

The shop owner Maurice warned her that it was an old-fashioned model and that one couldn't use it for taking quick snaps, but promised her that if she bought it he would teach her its secrets. Buying this particular type of camera, he said to her, was like buying an oud, but instead of playing with musical notes, one needed to learn how to play with light.

"It is a box of light, a machine that can see. If you buy it, I promise to teach you its secrets," he told her. And so, photographer Maurice explained to Dunya how her camera was no ordinary camera but an instrument—of light.

No child—let alone a girl—had ever bought a camera of that type since Maurice opened his shop, during the years of the French mandate, in 1943.

*

Patricia was happy that Dunya wanted to own something useful instead of merely another toy; it was proof that her daughter was finally growing up. But when she noticed that Dunya was developing an unhealthy attachment to her camera, that she even went to bed with it, she changed her mind.

From behind a crack in the door Patricia would observe Dunya pointing her camera at the night sky. She would point it at the air sometimes, sometimes at the wind. Instead of sleeping as she had been ordered to do, she would spend endless hours taking photographs of what seemed to Patricia to be nothing in particular.

In the end, Dunya confessed to her mother that she was trying to take a photograph of the moon, but that each time she tried to do so, the pale white circle of his face did not appear in her print.

"Who cares?" Patricia said to her daughter. "What is the point? Why don't you take photographs of me and of your father and your friends? Who cares about the moon? It is famously difficult to take a photograph of the moon, isn't it? You must start with something easier."

"I want to start with what's most difficult and then everything else will be easy," Dunya said. "You'll see."

Patricia noticed over time that Dunya seemed to be using her camera not only to take photographs of something as impossible as the face of the moon, but of many other impossible, even invisible, things. She seemed to be using her camera in a way that Patricia had not encountered before. She used it the way a scientist might use a telescope or a microscope, to discover and dissect things, as an instrument of curiosity, to document and prove and illustrate her eccentric ideas and illogical perceptions. Patricia was also concerned that playing with any type of mechanical object was not something that a girl should take too much to heart, particularly not a machine that made her *look*. Patricia believed that it was boys who looked, while girls should be looked at. A girl who looked was a contradiction in terms.

Why does she care about such headache-inducing things? Patricia often wondered to herself. *I do not understand it.* And instead of helping her to grow up into the sort of ladylike society girl that her parents wanted her to be, her obsession with her camera seemed to be worsening Dunya's tendency to escape from the real world and live in an imaginary one. Instead of spending her spare time shopping for dresses and shoes and looking at herself in a mirror, she only wanted to buy things for her camera. It was as if, from the moment she had found it, the world began to revolve around this silent seeing machine. It became her constant companion.

Dunya spent all her pocket money in Maurice's shop. Apart from providing her with black-and-white film rolls and lenses, he also opened her eyes to the powers that lay hidden in black-and-white photography and how to unlock them. The world in black and white might look like it is composed of only two colors, but in truth it is not so. And it can all be explained through a proper understanding of light.

Over the years Maurice taught Dunya the difference between black and white.

Black was hidden.

White was light.

But without some black and some white, one could not see the shape of things.

When Maurice developed a set of Dunya's negatives one day and found portraits of Joseph and Patricia in odd circumstances, he gasped in horror. Dunya had convinced Joseph, who was wearing a suit, to put a large bulb of garlic on his head and she tricked Patricia into wearing her cleaning lady's rose-studded peasant dress and to stand in front of a tall mirror holding a large eggplant in one of her hands, as if it were a handbag.

23

"Why don't you take normal photos of your family and friends? A bulb of garlic isn't a hat!" Maurice would advise, "An eggplant is not a bag."

"I know Maurice, but I like things to look *as if*."

Maurice often also worried about his protégée, as her approach did not seem purely craftsman-like. She seemed to want to use the camera to recreate the world in the way she wished it to be, or more alarmingly, as she imagined it to be. She didn't seem afraid of moving things from their proper locations and testing the effects of positioning them in unexpected places. The world as she wanted it to be was upside down; objects, people, and ideas were never where they were meant to be.

Now that they were well acquainted, Maurice would call Dunya "*darling*" and she would explain to him her latest idea for a photograph. "Just eyes, with no face, hair, or hat, nor a body. Yes. I love eyes. What do you think, Maurice?"

Maurice was quite surprised that such a young girl dared to treat him as a peer, to casually call him "Maurice," as if they were the same age, instead of calling him "Uncle Maurice," or "Sir," as all the other children did. "She seems to think everyone is equal. She can't see the differences between people. She's only interested in how they might appear in a photograph," Maurice grumbled to his wife. "She has no concept of social hierarchy." In Latakia there were strict hierarchies, and the hierarchy of adults and children was very strict. "You shouldn't encourage her," Maurice's wife would tell him. "You have your own children to bring up. Don't waste your time on other men's daughters."

Maurice told his wife things about Dunya every other day, but he wisely decided not to tell her about the time Dunya asked him to stand on his desk with a cup of coffee in his hand and to act as if that were normal, while she took a few shots of him. When a customer passed by, Maurice blushed, his coffee cup fell down and stained his new year's diary, and his blood pressure shot up to a dangerous degree.

Dunya often talked to Maurice about things she wouldn't have dreamed of discussing with her school friends, because she knew those things would only have bored them to tears. "You're such a dreamer!" he would tell her. But he enjoyed listening to her talking about things he secretly found quite intriguing and which busy and reality-bound adults in his social circle were too self-important and self-obsessed to have time for. Also, if they dared to talk about such things in Latakia they would have lost all respectability. In this town it was important to be regarded as someone whose feet were firmly planted on the ground.

"Don't you think taking photos is a little like fishing, you never know what kind of fish will turn up?" she asked.

As Dunya talked Maurice looked at her smiling, thinking to himself, *What kind of girl is this?* And then he told her, "I hope you're not going to become an artist. There's no bread in that. And you'll only suffer. Look at Van Gogh."

Dunya nodded. She had never heard of Van Gogh. The word 'Gogh' sounded exactly like the word 'plum' in Arabic, which made that sentence sound stranger to Dunya than it was.

"He cut one of his own ears off, you know, and posted it in an envelope!"

Dunya didn't understand.

5

The Truth About Love

THE CARMELITE SCHOOL FOR GIRLS, like every other school in Syria, was plastered with posters of Hero-President Hafez al-Assad, whose mustachioed face was used to ornament school notebooks, various textbooks, and the almost worthless lira coins. In the beginning, and to Patricia's silent horror, Dunya became a child victim of brainwashing by the state, swallowing whole the hero worship of President al-Assad, whom she idolized as if he were a pop star. Her political naivety was only matched by her budding religious faith, a faith that had been drummed into her by a cast of nun-trained religious education teachers. "Those who haven't been baptized will surely go to hell." Their teacher used to break this good news to them, while waving a stick in the air.

The Carmelite school had a separate religious education class for Muslim children, so that they could be spared the bad news. Christian children were often taught by fat women in black dresses (widows), while Muslims tended to have male teachers with strangely unfashionable brown suits and a mystical look in their eyes. They often wore silver wedding rings that were rumored to be a sign of membership of the Muslim Brotherhood—a secret and dangerous underground movement whose members promoted the growing of full beards rather than mustaches. They told their students in hushed voices that their non-Muhammad-loving friends were "infidels." And even though both groups believed everything their teachers told them while in the classroom, they forgot all about it and played together later, hiding the terrible truths they learned from one another.

In those early years, Dunya and most of her friends not only idolized and had blind faith in President Hafez al-Assad, but they also blindly believed in Jesus Christ, the Prophet Muhammad, and miracles.

"Faith is everything. Faith can move mountains," Maria Ghazi once tried to explain to Dunya. Maria was an especially religious child who tended to obsess about God, Jesus, and Mary even during history lessons. "Ask God for something and he will give it to you. But you need to have real faith, you must believe it will happen, otherwise it won't. He can read your mind so you mustn't just pretend. . . . You must really feel it," she whispered to Dunya.

"So if I ask him to send me an object, would that materialize in front of me here in the room . . . right now?" Dunya asked.

"Of course. Ask him for an apple, for instance—just to test him—and you'll see."

"Apple. Apple. God Almighty, send me an apple," Dunya mumbled and then waited. "Nothing's happening," she said.

"Do you one hundred percent *believe* that God will send you the apple?" Maria asked Dunya. "Try to really feel it, believe it, here, here."

She pointed at her own heart.

And sure enough, as soon as Dunya began to convince herself of the possibility that God would soon send her an apple, a huge red apple landed in her lap.

When the rather plump Madame Georgette saw Maria take an apple from a bag hidden under the table and throw it onto Dunya's lap, she came over with her long metal-centered cane and caned the two girls in front of a placid audience of pupils.

"I will ring your father if you carry on like this," Madame Georgette said with a mouth full of rice as Dunya was going out for lunch break. Madame Georgette often brought to school a Tupperware container full of stuffed zucchini, which she would eat angrily because she thought that children shouldn't be allowed such long lunch breaks.

Although the Carmelite School for Girls was supposed to be mainly for girls, boys were allowed to attend it until the age of eleven. After that it was considered that friendship between girls and boys was impossible and so the boys were swiftly packed off to a private boys' school called Kileye, where most of their fathers had also been indoctrinated in the arts of Syrian manhood and the highly evolved sciences of patriarchy.

It was around that time that Maria Ghazi's half blind grandmother Anaïs invited Maria and Dunya over for one of her regular preaching sessions and announced the following:

"I want to explain to you the truth about boys. It is a universal truth and whatever anyone else tells you, don't believe them! Listen to me carefully and etch these words in your brains. One day, you might accidentally look at a boy and he will smile at you; if you happen to be stupid enough to smile back at him, he will think that you love him. Boys are arrogant and vain. The boy will then begin to send you letters and slowly try to make you think *you* are in love with *him*. Don't ever believe him! Never look a boy in the eyes, and never smile at him, *never ever.* This is essential advice, my girls. Looking a boy in the eyes is always the beginning of a calamity. If you look at random boys and let yourselves be tricked, the most terrible things will happen. You will become a laughing stock. Even the boy himself will laugh at you and tell all his friends about how he caught you in his trap. Boys like that usually write letters to a number of girls all at once, to see which one will answer. These are not letters, they're bait. Boys are hunters and you're their prey."

"But don't boys fall in love too?"

"Sometimes they do, but most of the time they're lying. Don't ever believe a boy."

"What about granddad? How did you fall in love with granddad?" Maria asked.

"Fall in love? What are you talking about? Marriage is not about falling in love, my child. A sensible girl does not look for such things. No good marriage has ever been built on falling in love."

Although most of the boys who went to the Kiliye were from 'good families' that were well known and had been established in Latakia over many generations, only some of them were Christian, and it was only from that rather restricted pool of Christian boys that girls like Dunya and Maria would be allowed to choose a husband. And even if they couldn't give up the idea of love or didn't miraculously fall in love with one of these endangered species of boys, they would one day nevertheless be expected to marry one.

Despite his years in England, Joseph was as traditional and conservative as any other father in Syria. When he began to notice that Dunya was beginning to look at boys and be looked at, he wished he could hide her in a cupboard and let her out of the house only with armed protection.

One day, the greengrocer Kamil had the cheek to say to him, with a pained look in his eyes, "I've seen your daughter out with a boy called Malek, the son of a fisherman. And they were holding hands Dr. Noor, and he tells people she's his fiancée. . . ."

Dr. Noor felt a sense of deep shock and fear but pretended he didn't take Kamil seriously. Kamil the grocer didn't stop at that, however. He frowned and tut-tutted and added, "What will people think? And who will want to marry your daughter in the future, if she is seen with a boy like that? Also, she still wears shorts, Dr. Noor. Most girls stop wearing shorts by the time they're ten. She's almost a young lady now. She shouldn't be exposing so much leg. Maybe her mother thinks we're in England, but we're not, Dr. Noor."

If a lowly shopkeeper like Kamil thought it fit to be giving Dr. Noor advice on how to bring up his daughter, then things were really getting out of hand. And Dunya was not yet twelve.

That afternoon, Joseph sent one of his more stocky male nurses to Malek's house to slap him once or twice on the face and tell him to keep his filthy, fishy hands off Dunya. "Who do you think you are?" the nurse demanded, after he slapped Malek a third time and threatened to report him to the police if he saw him with Dunya again. "Boys like you should be whipped. Next time I will have you whipped, do you hear me?"

For many weeks after that incident Dunya was grounded, her bedroom was searched for love letters and photographs, any traces of the dangerous arsenal that boys used in their campaigns to ensnare unsuspecting girls. Dunya insisted that she was not, and never had been, in love with Malek, but no one believed her.

Dunya had met Malek when she was trying to understand the truth about love. Granny Anaïs' version did not ring true to her. Instead of avoiding love, she wanted to discover exactly what it was and why everyone was so scared of it; why was it seen as such a dangerous and dark force that must be combatted at all cost?

And so, in addition to her interest in her camera, the only other thing that captured Dunya's heart in those early years was the idea of love. She thought about it and read about it, and she talked about it with Maria over and over again. They secretly read love poetry to one another to try and discover the truth. Dunya could not believe that the people who had written these poems, many of whom were men, were lying.

They had both heard that when love occurred, the object of one's love would begin to sparkle and then he would look as if he were bathed in light. It was then that a girl's heartbeats would accelerate and she would soon feel as if she had grown a pair of wings.

On the day Dunya met Malek, she had seen him looking at her with his dark eyes that were framed by his long, dark eyelashes. She looked back at him and smiled. Then she waited to see if anything would happen. Would she? Wouldn't she? Did she? Didn't she?

In her intensive researches about love, Dunya had come to the conclusion that what Granny Anaïs had said was partly true, that looking at boys and being looked at was the first and most guaranteed way to fall in love. But she also discovered something new that no one had ever revealed to her or to Maria before, which was that real love, the most intense and life-altering variety, was the sort where one loved a boy and was loved by him at first sight—without words having been spoken or letters received or exchanged. Love at first sight was produced when twin souls happened to look into each other's eyes.

But instead of experiencing the pain and pleasure of falling in love when she saw Malek, Dunya caused a scandal. And from then on, society women always talked about her and her fisher-boy lover—which was not a good reputation to acquire at such an early age. Falling in love with *any* boy was seen as a tremendous criminal offense in those days, but to fall in love with a fisherman's son—that was beyond anyone's understanding.

6

The Dangers of Nodding

PATRICIA KNEW THAT HER DAUGHTER would never be able to follow these restrictive rules of love and she dreaded the prospect of having to keep an eye on Dunya in a city where most men were regarded as forbidden fruit. She was still convinced, however, that Joseph was bound to realize that there was no future for Dunya here. "Latakia is so backward that it doesn't even have its own supermarket, for God's sake!" she often scolded him.

Well, apart from Rafi's Supermarket, which was more of a corner shop and whose only claim to the status of a *super*-market was that it had a cash register—something unheard of in other shops. It was the only place in the whole length and breadth of Latakia that sold quite a few illegal foreign foods, such as English baked beans, Italian mortadella, Chinese canned meats, French mayonnaise, Australian bacon, French La Vache Qui Rit (or Laughing Cow) cheese, the more serious Kiri cheese, and baking powder made in the United States, all of which had to be especially smuggled in from Lebanon. Rafi's shop had a decidedly foreign air, which was enough to glamorize it into a 'super' existence.

Rafi had also begun to make a name for himself as an unofficial real estate agent, as there were no real estate agencies in Latakia during that period.

"If we decide to move back to England, Rafi, do you think you could sell our house for us?" Patricia asked him.

"Are you going back to England, Madame?" Rafi asked with awe. The idea of a country like England filled him with admiration; he had heard it was full of huge, nay, gigantic supermarkets that were so enormous one could drive a car through their aisles. He also heard that instead of being served, customers in England were trusted to pick whatever items or products that took their fancy *with their own hands* and pile them up in large metal carts. An army of uniformed staff (wearing name badges and hats) were employed to refill shelves and operate cash registers. Oh, England, England! England was so high-tech and civilized. It was a veritable Vatican for devotees of supermarkets. (Rafi was Armenian and also a devout Catholic.)

Patricia nodded smugly.

Rafi was impressed. What an honor it was for him to be speaking to a real English woman and one who looked like such a lady. Just looking at Patricia reminded him of the glamour of cinema, the beauty of blond hair, compared to the ugliness around him.

"We won't sell for less than one million lira. Do you know people who might be interested when the time comes?" Patricia said with her heavily accented Arabic. Rafi wished his wife was English too and that she spoke Arabic with such a seductive accent. No house had ever been worth a million Syrian Lira at that point in history. Patricia was so posh that Rafi wondered whether he should bow to her.

"I will find out for you, Madame Noor. Leave it to me, I will find you someone. Perhaps a princess from the Gulf will be able to afford it. I'll spread the word."

"Keep the matter under wraps, Rafi. Would you consider it too English of me to ask you to sign a confidentiality agreement? I don't want my husband to hear of this yet."

Rafi looked at Patricia and smiled. He plucked a hair off his mustache and handed it to her. "This is my confidentiality agreement; a man's word is his honor."

Patricia quietly put the valuable mustache hair in a safe pocket in her handbag.

The next day Rafi inspected Mr. and Mrs Noor's penthouse apartment, while taking notes. "Ahem," he said. This looked like the sort of home people in Latakia only saw on TV. It was full of exquisite velvet curtains, expensive blue Chinese porcelain, rosewood statues, and the scent of freshly cut flowers. Rafi had often heard rumors about how it was strangely arranged on two floors, something unheard of in Latakia, and today he saw with his own eyes that this was true. He whistled in admiration.

There was no other apartment or house in the city of Latakia with an indoor staircase, with the bedrooms, en-suite bathrooms, and a second lounge upstairs. It was on the seventh floor but also on the sixth floor. That was quite a selling point. The views of the harbor from so high up were breathtaking, though this also had its drawbacks in Latakia, where the electricity supply was very erratic and visitors were often too scared to take the elevator and preferred to walk up the dark staircase. But Rafi was not going to mention this in his report.

Almost every wall in the Noors' home was covered with mirrors; hundreds of mirrors of the sort and type Rafi had never seen before, the sort one might find in royal palaces or international museums. He had heard once that Patricia Noor was responsible for at least ten percent of all antique mirror sales in the Republic of Syria and some people had claimed that she was a mirror addict. Yes, they said, Patricia liked to sneak glimpses at herself as she walked around her apartment, to keep an eye on her most important assets (and who wouldn't if they looked like that?). But there was another, deeper truth—that some of her female friends had gleaned from her and gossiped about—which was that Patricia *needed* the mirrors to survive. Living in a foreign city Patricia was afraid she would one day forget who she was, were she not to constantly remind herself by looking in the mirror.

Rafi's heart bled for Patricia. *How could a woman like her live in a city like ours?* he thought. *It must be love,* he realized, *she must really love Joseph.*

By the time Dunya had reached the delicate age of thirteen things had begun to change. The school uniform was now basically a miniature military outfit, complete with shoes, epaulets, and military cap. A new class appeared on the curriculum: the Youth Military Education class, every Wednesday afternoon, taught by Miss Huda, a twenty-two-year old despot with scary contacts in the Baath Party and extra-black kohl that she used to enhance her terror-inducing eyes.

Miss Huda came in one day and told her pupils they had to go on a demonstration the next day whether they were ill, feverish, or had broken bones, whether their mothers had collectively died or their houses were on fire, *or else!* Dunya decided then and there that she wasn't going to go. It was not the first time this kind of threat had been made and Dunya always joined in the compulsory 'voluntary' marches. She and everyone at the school would stand passively in the playground without daring to utter a syllable.

While one could hear a pin drop, Miss Huda and a band of disturbed-looking assistants would furnish everyone in the school with a placard chock-a-block with angry anti-American and anti-Zionist slogans. Since everyone, including children and teenagers, agreed that Palestine should be liberated and that Palestinians needed to get their homes back, she didn't understand why they had to be forced to march, or why they were not allowed to write their own placards. The venom, humiliation, and rule by fear were beginning to disturb her. Although she was only just a teenager, living in a politicized country meant that Dunya had often heard the word "freedom," but when she added two and two together her calculation was that there was zero freedom in Syria. She saw how her generation was being bullied into submission for no reason that she could understand. The buzzwords everywhere were democracy, freedom of speech, and liberation. There were constant claims that the Baath (or Renaissance) Party had finally given those precious gifts to the people of Syria and how everyone was deeply joyous, but it soon dawned on Dunya that this was just a lie.

"A lie, a lie, a lie," she told Maria.

"Sh, sh, sh," Maria replied.

"I won't go to the demonstration."

"You're just saying that. You can't *not* go. Don't be silly, Dunya."

When Dunya fulfilled her promise to Maria and didn't turn up to the march as she and all the other children had been ordered to do, she did not know that this was going to be the beginning of the end of her life as a Syrian child.

What really put the nail in the coffin of her short-lived childhood in Syria was her refusal to apologize for her absence, and her refusal to make up an excuse for it. She also categorically refused to accept the harsh punishment of crawling like a caterpillar along the cement playground, and when Miss Huda asked her, "Is this because you are against the Baath Party?"

Dunya nodded.

"Yes? Did you say yes? Say it, say it to me to my face, say the word! Are you *against* our *great* Baath Party?"

"Yes," Dunya said.

A frozen silence filled the air. Miss Huda's strange, blow-dried hair seemed to stand on end. She simply couldn't believe her eyes or ears. No one, *no one* in the whole length and breadth of the Democratic Republic of Syria in their right mind would dare utter such a blasphemy.

Miss Huda wanted to slap Dunya across the face and flatten her, as she usually did with pupils whenever an opportunity presented itself, but she decided to restrain herself and to go instead to the local headquarters of the Baath Party to discuss the matter. She and most of her peers at the Party were convinced that if spoiled children like Dunya Noor were allowed to express such dissent, without undergoing public humiliation and punishment, the revolution would lose its authority. It must never be allowed.

"You will be crucified for this, Dunya Noor. You watch," Miss Huda said, and walked off in her cheap white heels and her military outfit, which she wore in a figure-hugging style that added a strange, tatty glamour to her generally menacing appearance.

The next day all of Latakia was breathless to find out whether Dunya Noor would be arrested for nodding in the wrong direction. But Patricia had already packed her and her daughter's suitcases and taken a taxi all the way to Damascus Airport.

Dunya walked onto the airplane carrying a small red suitcase, with her old black camera around her neck. She was still not sure what this meant. Why did she have to be flown out of the country because she said that she didn't like the Baath Party? Is liking something compulsory? Do you have to pretend that you love something you hate in order not to be flown out of the country? Why did the government care so much whether people loved them or not? And why did they feel that they had to resort to the use of force to get this love that they so craved?

"They all just need a bath," she said to Patricia in English as the bossy-looking, multilingual stewardess gave her a blanket and a small cushion and perked up her ears to try and catch the gist of the conversation. Many stewardesses doubled up as intelligence agents to earn extra cash, and a tall foreign woman with a quirky, naughty-looking, curly haired Syrian daughter was not an everyday sight on these night flights.

"I do wish you didn't have such a big mouth, Dunya. Don't you understand we are living under a dictatorship? Do you not understand what this means? Keep your voice down, Dunya. If the stewardess hears you, we'll be flown back in no time!" she whispered anxiously as the Syrian Arab Airways plane buzzed its way across Europe, heading toward the island that was a kingdom and Queen Elizabeth's home.

So, thought Dunya, *if one expresses one's true opinion, one either gets flown out of the country or flown back to it?*

That night Joseph lay in bed and stared at the ceiling. When dawn broke he waited a few hours until it was a decent time to ring Mr. Ghazi, and in a hot-headed moment of fear he agreed to sell him his precious penthouse apartment. Then he packed his suitcase and prepared to escape the country, fearing his career would be tarnished by the revelation that his daughter was an anti-establishment figure. But only a few moments before he left his home the phone rang. It was one of his old clients: an influential Baath Party official whose heart he had rescued from certain explosion a couple of years back.

"Dr. Noor," he said. "We know you're leaving and we know that your daughter and wife have already left. We could've stopped them if we'd wanted to and we can stop you too—you must know that—but we didn't and we won't. Do you know why?"

"No," said Dr. Noor.

"It is because you saved my life all those years ago. And now it is time for me to save your and your daughter's life. You don't have to leave your homeland, Dr. Noor, if you don't want to. All my colleagues want from you is to make sure that Dunya never ever opens her mouth again. Surely you can control your own daughter?" the official said gently. And then he added, "Also she will have to publicly apologize to Miss Huda in front of the whole school and crawl up and down on her arms and legs across the playground fifty times. This is not much to ask, is it? She's a lucky girl, Joseph, because she's your daughter," the official said.

"Thank you, my dear brother," Dr. Noor said. "You are a true friend."

Since he had already given his word to his friend Ghazi, there was no way Joseph could ask for his penthouse apartment back and keep his manly honor, so he pretended that he was planning to get rid of it anyway and that he had never had any plans to leave the country. He cancelled his flight to London and within days he'd bought another two glitzy apartments that were built one above the other across the road. He planned to link them up later with an internal staircase, thus reproducing his unique duplex (with extra large balconies), and giving his friend Salman Ghazi another inferiority complex.

He unpacked his boxes and suitcases in the new apartment and drank some black coffee. That same afternoon, Joseph moved all the family furniture in, with the eager help of Mr. Ghazi and his son George, as well as a bunch of young men who had not yet reached their prime.

When Patricia arrived at her parents' house in Surrey, her father Cyril smiled a deep paternal smile. He was too polite to say, "I told you so," but her mother Sally sighed a loud sigh of relief in celebration of her daughter and granddaughter's return to the civilized world, where children were allowed to have political opinions without fear of being locked up—a freedom which caused them to lose all interest in politics.

Patricia's attempts at luring Joseph back to England failed once again, and, in no time, Joseph managed to convince her to come back to Syria, simply by writing her a postcard:

Darling Patricia,
1. I can't live without you.
2. You can't make me choose between you and my country.
3. I am needed here.

4. There are millions of doctors in London.
5. I need to stay.
6. Come back, my sweetheart.

After seven weeks of being a mother in England, Patricia booked her flight back to continue her life as a wife in Syria. Both Joseph and Patricia decided that it was safer for Dunya to stay in England, for how could anyone be sure she would not open her mouth and tell the truth again?

7

England

DUNYA'S GRANDMOTHER SALLY SPENT MOST of her days in the
garden where she bred many species of flowers and plants.
She loved roses most of all, which she pruned and fed and
watered in an elegant Victorian greenhouse.

After Patricia, her only daughter, abandoned England
and her aging and long-suffering parents—all because Joseph
said so—Sally consoled herself with Dunya, whom she saw as
a new species of rose, one she was going to set about implant-
ing in English soil. Sally noticed how, since Dunya's arrival
in England, her curls were drooping, her eyes were losing the
brightness of their light, and she suddenly stopped laughing—
almost overnight.

It was incomprehensible to Sally how her son-in-law
Joseph could put his love for his country ahead of his love
for his wife and daughter. Even after what had happened to
Dunya, he preferred to pretend that it was all her fault rather
than face the fact that his country was ruled by a bunch of
insecure men who couldn't handle criticism, even from a
little girl. Sally had often wished that Joseph was English,
because then, she reasoned, he would've been more sensible.
It was Joseph's fault that Dunya, her only granddaughter,
was neither English, nor sensible. Sally tried everything to
find a method by which to turn Dunya into an English rose,
but after countless attempts, she finally realized that it was
going to be impossible.

"Come and sit on the sofa, my darling, next to us," Sally said to Dunya every time she caught her sitting under a table with her back to the radiator.

"I'll knit you a thicker jumper and you'll never be cold again," Sally held Dunya in her arms.

But however many jumpers Dunya wore, she always felt cold in England. Even while sitting next to the fire, she felt cold. Even when it became warm outside, she continued to feel the cold inside. And when she covered her heart with the palm of her hand, she could feel the cold there too.

"Perhaps if I make you a bowl of porridge, my darling, every morning." Sally said, "you'll begin to feel warm."

"Perhaps," Dunya said in the old-fashioned, cut-glass English accent Patricia had taught her.

"This, my darling, is a spoon for you. I've engraved your name on it." Cyril handed Dunya a beautifully designed silver spoon. "With it you must eat your morning porridge and soon you'll be as right as rain."

Cyril was a keen spoon collector and had a room full of spoons in every shape and size: silver, tin, gold, copper, ladles, teaspoons, Italian spoons, Syrian spoons, French spoons, adult, and baby spoons. Any sort of spoon was of intense interest to him. And he didn't just collect for the sake of collecting. He collected in order to try and find a pattern, to see something, to understand.

"Lie down on the carpet, Granddad, I would like to take a photograph of you. We can then post it to Mama, as a souvenir."

Cyril lay down on the floor in his study on an old rug. "Why do you like spoons so much, Granddad?" Dunya asked him, arranging his silvery locks of hair in a pattern she found pleasing. She rested a brown bowler hat on his head and made him hold a long black umbrella in his right hand.

Cyril answered in his textured Queen's English baritone, while staring dreamily at the ceiling. "I like spoons because they help me understand human nature. Spoons, my dear child, symbolize the modern English, the new spirit of England. We are a Nation of the Spoon!"

Dunya opened one of Cyril's glass cabinets and took out one spoon at a time. She positioned them in a strange formation, some like a halo around his bowler hat, others next to his ears and the rest distributed around his outstretched arms. She climbed onto a chair and began to take one photograph after the other of her grandfather Cyril and as she photographed him, Cyril told her about the historical case of Spoon Fixation in Anglo-Saxon societies. "We are obsessed with spoon-bending, spoon-feeding, children born with silver spoons in their mouths, and those who were born with tin spoons. We are plagued by greed, and the need for bigger and better spoons, a national wish to devour and grow. We're plagued with physical plenty yet the need to gobble more things up. And why? It is to fill the hole in our hearts, my darling, the terrible emptiness!" Cyril said. "England found its head years ago, but in the process it lost its heart. In your country it is the opposite."

Only Cyril seemed to understand why it was so difficult for Dunya to be happy in the rational world of England, where logic ruled and magic had been forgotten, where facts were collected but meaning had been lost, where it was not only tomatoes, roses, trees, grass, but also children that were made to grow too fast, whose dreams and illusions were not allowed to last.

At school, English teenagers of her age thought of themselves as fully fledged adults and appeared to be fixated on sex, but never mentioned love. The idea of spiritual love, where one becomes besotted with another's soul through gazing into their eyes, did not make any sense to them, because (they said) it wasn't scientifically proven. *Anything that cannot be proved by science does not exist.* When Dunya mentioned "spiritual love" to one of her classmates, a girl whose name was Samantha, the girl wondered whether Dunya had taken to the bottle or was deeply into Ouija boards. When she mentioned the word "soul," Samantha thought she meant the fish.

Her school friends' attention seemed to be focused—laser-beam like—on the intricate and intimate personal lives of the Higher Beings who peopled TV soap operas and the worlds of pop and rock. To someone from a softer and warmer culture like Syria's it seemed incomprehensible that being hard and 'rock-like' was a desirable asset in England and that being 'cool' was considered such a must-have quality for social and even romantic success. England's view of the world was upside down, and the qualities she'd been brought up to cherish were equated here on the British Isles with weakness.

And so, instead of only worshipping one god (Hafez al-Assad, Jesus, or Muhammad), young people here had the option of worshipping a vast array of sex gods, who were invariably either members of the Pop Aristocracy or Soap Luminaries. They also had the option of worshipping themselves. Instead of being pressurized and almost forced to be exactly the same as one another (like in Syria), English teenagers tried instead to find themselves by becoming special, unique, and 'individual.' But when Dunya discovered that most of these 'individuals' had found their own brand of individuality in a magazine—by slavishly copying one of a hundred or so role model options—her disillusion was complete. Glossy magazines were the manuals that competed like gospels to provide the masses with a guide to that Other Life that everyone craved so badly. The bank manager was the newly ordained priest.

In Britain, the supermarket seemed to have become more important than the church and the British Isles soon seemed to Dunya more like a gigantic shop than a country. Everything had a price tag and a label.

It was hard, almost impossible, for her to try and adjust to the temperatures, both physical and metaphysical, of what seemed to her a sub-zero climate, an emotionally frozen island that prided itself on being a PLC.

Was freedom, then, just the freedom to shop? Dunya wondered during that time. Or was it also the freedom to open your mouth and say whatever you liked without anyone taking any notice of you?

Yes, she was technically fifty percent English. Her feet were in England, her head was in England, her nose was in England, her eyes were in England, and her hair was in England.

But she had left her heart in Syria.

BOOK TWO
The Tailor's Son

How did the only son of a tailor in Aleppo grow up to be a boy who dared to dream?

8

The History of Hilal

HILAL WAS A RARE NAME in Syria, and despite its poetic meaning (crescent moon), due to obscure historical and social evolutions, most people had come to consider it archaic and low class. He was the son of an idealistic and mild-mannered tailor and a soft-hearted seamstress who had set up business in Aleppo in 1970 after they were forced to flee from their small village in the south of Syria. Tailoring had been in Hilal's family since his great-great-great-grandfather Hisham Kamil Shihab set up a tailoring practice in 1880, making uniforms for the Ottoman army that ruled Syria until 1922.

It was no mystery why Hilal did not become a tailor. His parents had noticed how clumsy their son was with needles and how hopeless with a sewing machine. They had also noticed that he had a terrible sense of color coordination and concluded that because of all this he would be a mediocre dress designer. But if Hilal wasn't going to take over their successful His & Hers Sewing Atelier on Plum Street, who was going to?

When Hilal received the highly coveted Aleppo University Physics Prize, which included a full postgraduate grant to study in London, both his parents cried with happiness. Hilal couldn't understand why they were suddenly so happy when they knew that they might now lose him for almost four years and possibly even longer. Wasn't he their only son, the apple of their eyes? Hilal knew that his mother had her doubts about his studies as she had no idea what kind of career path they would lead him to. He'd explained to her that he wanted to become an astronomer who specializes in the moon and that his dream was to set up Syria's first astronomical observatory. He told her how the first astronomers were Arab and how they had studied the moon and used it as a calendar and that he now wanted to make a contribution to this science. He wanted to discover new things about the moon and then write a paper about it.

This did not make sense to Suad and, in fact, it worried her, for although the moon and the stars were beautiful to look at, she could not understand how anyone could make a living from studying them or writing papers about them, papers consisting mainly of numbers and symbols. What was the use of such activity and who would give him a job doing this? And could the son of such humble people as her and Said dare to dream such impossible dreams or think that he could ever be paid a salary to spend his time theorizing and writing equations about, of all things, the moon? Who did he think he was? Syria was a poor country where people needed bread, not obscure and irrelevant information about an alluring object in the sky. Shouldn't Hilal become a physics teacher or a doctor or an architect or even, in the worst-case scenario, a poet? In a country like Syria, poetry was more useful than astronomy. At least it filled people's hearts. Was he not setting himself up for failure and disappointment by trying to reach for the stars? Suad often thought these thoughts but never dared to speak them out loud, for theirs was a family where silence spoke louder than words and where actions were substitutes for verbs.

Neither she nor Said were in the habit of asking their son too many questions, for he had always been the secretive type and they had both always encouraged this quality in him because they were even more secretive than he. They were also rather afraid that if they dared to ask Hilal personal questions, he would start asking them questions too, the answers to which they had been trying to hide from him since he was born.

A simple question that Hilal had often wished he could ask both his parents was, "Why are you so unhappy?"

They could not tell him the answer to that and nor could they tell him that now, secretly in their hearts, they were indeed temporarily happy—as he had suspected—because he was going to live in London (or as they called it: "Landun"). Since his birth, their hearts had often quaked with fear for their son. His going to London was maybe for the best, because London was as far away from the map of his destiny as could be.

According to their neighbor Farida, who was known to read the future fluently in coffee cups, something would one day cause their son a devastating loss, something more obscure than run-of-the-mill diseases or the universal condition of mortality. He is not ill, she'd told them but ill-fated. "The probability was high," she'd said and had also claimed that it was in Aleppo that ill fate awaited Hilal around every corner. And although no one knew exactly what this ill fate looked like, both Suad and Said had been categorically told and given definite proof that in this instance, for Hilal, it would come in the shape of a girl.

The source of his parents' unhappiness became more and more of a mystery to Hilal as the years went by. He knew certain things about them. He knew for example that Said was descended from a family of Sunni Muslim tailors, while Suad belonged to a family of Alawite Muslim tailors, and that for generations both groups of tailors had made sure that their children never married one another. If they'd ever tried to (or even dared to contemplate it), the punishments were always brutal. Ostracism, banishment, and sometimes murder were the fates of those who disobeyed.

Hilal knew that he was born to a couple on the run. He knew that they'd had to flee and that they'd hidden in the heart of the city of Aleppo in a small apartment above a soap shop where no one could find them, where they still lived to this day. He'd heard how they'd brought with them a sewing machine, two excellent pairs of scissors, and a collection of measuring tapes. And how very soon after their arrival, word had spread around the ancient souk that a nineteen-year-old tailor and seamstress of unknown origin had set up a workshop in their rented apartment, making dresses and suits that were the envy of Aleppo.

No one understood how a young couple from an obscure village in the south could produce such stylish designs that made the poorest and least attractive woman look like she was blessed with both looks and money, or how their suits made men appear taller and more distinguished. A man wearing one of their suits looked like a man with prospects, it was said. And so it was that many men who wanted to convince their potential in-laws to grant them their daughter's hand in marriage would come and order one of their suits, as well as scores of men who wanted to cut important business deals. Lovers, wannabes, and charlatans became their regular customers, as well as social climbers, self-promoters, and diva types, both male and female. This was in addition to regular run-of-the-mill folk, who just needed an outfit and were not expecting to see themselves so transformed after their innocent visit to His & Hers Sewing Atelier.

Ironically, Said hardly ever wore suits himself and was often seen wearing a simple pair of trousers and a white shirt without a tie, and Suad always wore a black dress, something that was very unusual. Only women who were in mourning wore black in Syria. The only time Said and Suad ever dressed up in fancy outfits was on their wedding day, which no one had attended apart from themselves and the young sheikh who signed the register and who wore a robe and a turban. Afterward, the couple had visited a photographer and had their first ever photograph taken. This photograph fascinated Hilal for years and provided him with more clues and evidence that something must have happened to his parents *after* their marriage. This photograph showed him very clearly how happy his parents once were. The expression on their faces was of pure joy and intense love, the sort of expression that could not be faked. Their photograph was almost ablaze, their faces seemed to ignite, their bodies almost alight. Hilal couldn't understand what it was that had happened to his parents since that time. Since he could remember them, they had seemed like a couple who had lost something precious and could not recover from their loss. Why did they look so disappointed and so full of fear and anxiety when they had managed to achieve instant acceptance and success upon their arrival at this vast city and when they had made such a name for themselves in one of the most bustling and competitive souks in the region?

The mystery behind their unhappiness could not be that their love had faded, because they still seemed deeply attached to one another. Theirs was a strange love that did not seem to fade like many other loves did.

Although Said was a naturally handsome man who possessed exquisitely romantic eyes, which caused almost all his female clients to become determined to seduce him somehow or another, Said only seemed to have eyes for his wife. Many took it personally and disliked Suad for her hold on him and envied her such love. They even resented seeing her so unhappy as they could not understand how she could be so with a devoted husband like him by her side. It was a mystery to all (not only Hilal) why, with all the blessings that they appeared to possess, Mr. and Mrs. Shihab hardly ever smiled. It became clear to all who met them that Said and Suad were the sort of couple that one sometimes heard about or saw in tragic films and novels. No one knew their true story, nor the source of their woe. Hilal knew that Suad often cried in secret, because her mascara always ran and, as they didn't have mirrors in the house, she didn't notice and did not wipe away the tears that betrayed her.

Hilal also noticed that his mother never did any sewing any more, that she was always planning to make a beautiful yellow dress, thinking about it, mentioning it, but that she never actually sewed. She dreamed of this dress, and even produced drawings of it. But it was never perfect enough, and so the burden of the His & Hers Sewing Atelier fell squarely upon his father's rather wide shoulders. Gradually Hilal became convinced that he was not imagining things and that his parents' silence enveloped a mystery that he was purposely excluded from.

When he was a boy, it was rare for Hilal to see the sky at night; inside the bustling covered alleys of the Aleppo souk the sky seemed irrelevant.

At the age of nine or ten Hilal saw the sky in full for the first time, when his father took him to see the Aleppo citadel. And up there, at sunset, he saw the sun disappearing gradually on the right side and on the left a shape drawn in white appeared.

"What is this?" he asked his father.

"This is a *hilal*, a crescent moon."

"A Hilal?" He jumped up. "What do you mean a Hilal? I thought *I* was a Hilal. . . ."

"It is your namesake, my darling," his father said. "I named you after it, didn't you know?"

"No, I didn't know, Dad. Does it appear every evening?"

"Sometimes it does and other times it does not. It looks different every night. It grows a little wider until it becomes a circle and then it continues to diminish until it disappears. Half of the month it's not there. Have you never seen it, my son?" Said looked at him with pity and concern.

"No." Hilal ran to the highest point of the citadel and stared up into the sky.

"I'm a terrible father. How did I forget to show you the moon?" Said pulled him close.

There was a world up there no one knew about, a world whose mystery caught him by the lapels. Hilal's look of distraction and his habit of asking questions and living in his own head became something that he would never outgrow, something that became a part of him. And now, instead of looking at his parents and asking questions, he began to look at the sky and take notes. He read every book he could find about science, astronomy, poetry, philosophy, myth, geometry, and gradually discovered the beauty and mystery of numbers.

When Hilal was fourteen he made his first reflecting telescope. But when he went up on the roof to test it at night, all the men of the neighborhood went up in arms, thinking he might use it to spy on their wives and daughters. They made him swear he'd never use it in the vicinity of the city of Aleppo, so he hid it in a box.

From then on, on two Friday afternoons a month Hilal would pack some sandwiches and take a bus into the countryside and wait for evening to fall. He wouldn't come back home until the next morning, with his hair full of dust.

Just as Hilal used to look at his mother and father and wonder at what their silence hid, they too looked at him.

"Does he love a girl, do you think?" his father Said used to whisper in his wife's ear.

"Those dreamy eyes of his never reveal anything," Suad said.

Most boys in Aleppo at that age had seen a girl whom they would never be allowed to speak to and with whom they fell in love at first sight. Perhaps, Said thought, his son was suffering from such a predicament too. At any one time in Syria, thousands of boys were busy writing poems for the object of their love and contemplating her beauty and all the virtues they imagined her to have. It was always this girl (the object of their undying love, the idol of their young hearts) whom they secretly thought about when they were silent or writing notes in their notebooks. Most boys in Aleppo were forced to become poets out of necessity, as a result of never being allowed to love the girl they gave their hearts to. Said often watched his son sitting at his desk during the evenings, filling an ever-growing number of notebooks with writings from his silver fountain pen, notebooks that he then locked in a box and took with him to London.

9

The Moonologist

IT WAS PERHAPS THE WAY his hair curled just so or the way the white lapels of his shirt turned to the left and to the right, like *this* or like *that*. He seemed like a man from another era, almost. Or maybe it was the way he held his silver fountain pen and moved it across the pages of his book from right to left with such love and satisfaction, while he underlined certain sentences, or maybe it was the look of intense concentration and delight that she saw on his handsome face, while he flicked its pages one by one. Its title—she could see it: *A Biography of the Moon*—was printed in Arabic.

It was such an innocent thing to do and Dunya had done it so many times before. She looked down into the viewfinder of her old-style camera and began to observe her subject more closely.

He was wearing an elegant sky blue suit, the sort that very few young men still wore (and in Dunya's lexicon of colors, blue had always been the color of dreams). And although his suit was exquisite, his hair (which was pitch-black) was un-brushed and very curly. He was unshaven and he didn't seem like someone who was particularly fashion-conscious or vain. He had the aura of a man who didn't live in this world, but in the world of the imagination.

Dunya couldn't focus her lens properly, nor could she decide what shutter speed she needed to take the right sort of photograph of him, or what aperture. Instead she just stared: at his hair, at his eyes, at his suit, at his hands, and at his book. Every time she looked at him she felt her heart jump. His beautiful dark eyes sometimes moved in her direction and she could stare directly into them—without him guessing it. His apparent familiarity baffled her: had she met him before? She thought about it, and tried to remember when it might've been, until she realized that it was never.

He raised his head and looked in her direction again. Dunya pressed the shutter button, and then began to pack her things, but he was already walking in her direction.

"Good morning," he said.

"Good morning," Dunya answered and then she went bright red. "I'm sorry that . . ." she said.

"That what?"

"Well that I took a photo of you, without asking."

"I don't understand. You don't even have a camera on you. Anyway, I just came to ask you the time."

Dunya blushed again.

"Well, unless your camera is invisible," he continued.

"It is invisible," she pointed at a box next to her on a wall. "And I don't have a watch."

Hilal examined the box and saw a circle on its side that faced toward his bench. Then he looked at its top and saw the old-fashioned viewfinder. "What a clever contraption. It's like an earthly telescope," he said. "Why did you want a photo of me, have I become a celebrity overnight?"

"I wasn't taking a photograph of you particularly. I don't know you," Dunya said. "I come here every day at this time and I take a photograph of whoever might be sitting on this bench. Today was my last day, then I will have an exhibition."

"And will you invite me to it?" he asked. His voice touched her in a strange, almost physical way. It traveled through the air in definite and speedy steps, in a straight line to her heart.

At that moment it was impossible for Dunya not to feel that this must be him, that it could only be him: *no one but him.*

*

The next day Hilal turned up to her house to pick up a copy of his photograph.

"I'm a scientist of the moon," he told her, sipping tea out of her favorite yellow porcelain cup.

"I study the properties of moonlight and how it might help us discover hidden objects in the sky and make the invisible visible," he said.

"But this sounds far too poetic to be scientific," Dunya said.

"Science and poetry are one and the same; they should've never been separated. I'm a scientist of the old school, I still believe in miracles, and that life has a meaning and a purpose. I look for it in the stars, while poets look for it in their hearts."

"So in other words you're more of a Moonologist?" Dunya smiled at Hilal.

"A Moon-*ologist*? Well, yes, I suppose you could call me that," Hilal smiled back.

What a girl, this Dunya was. She truly was the sort of girl he'd never imagined he'd meet. So unlike any other.

When Hilal first discovered Dunya he felt as if he'd discovered a new and unexpected star in the sky while gazing through his telescope. He wanted to jump up and down and proclaim to the world: "I have found her! I have discovered her! *She* whom they told me did not exist."

It only took him two more minutes to realize that he had fallen head over heels in love with Dunya, and he could not quite explain how and why it happened. No scientist, no poet, no policeman, nor detective, would have the wherewithal necessary to pinpoint exactly why, out of all the girls in the world that he'd met so far, his heart so unexpectedly and so unpredictably and so impulsively chose Dunya. Yes, she was pretty; yes, she seemed like an original, a one-off. But he had hardly spoken to her, he knew nothing about her; to all intents and purposes she was a complete stranger. Despite this, he could

61

not stop that flood, that overwhelming, blinding feeling that took his heart and soul and his entire body prisoner.

By the time Hilal grasped the full implications of his terrible predicament—it was too late.

What if she didn't love him back? What if she brushed him off like a mosquito or a fly? What if she laughed in his face, what if, worse than all of the above, she pitied him? How dangerous it was to lose one's heart like this, not step by step, but instantly and not by choice. Perhaps the sensible thing to do, he decided, was to hide his feelings from her. Many girls were scared of love, as were most men. A love like this he'd heard took courage. And now for the first time in his life, Hilal understood why. He must look at her sideways, not directly, he must not look her in the eyes, he must put on a show of indifference, keep his cards close to his chest—that was the clever thing to do, in circumstances like these.

Dunya stood up and went to her darkroom and came back with a large envelope, which she handed to Hilal.

When he opened it he found a hand-printed, black-and-white photograph of his face. Not even his hair was visible, only his face and everything in it. And a *light*. Yes, there was a clear light that made visible the thing in him that he most wanted to hide—not only from Dunya, but also mostly from himself.

Oh no! He couldn't keep looking at it; it was the terrifying light of love in his eyes, irrevocable proof and evidence— strong enough to be accepted in a court of law—that he had fallen in love with the girl who had taken that photograph of him. How could she not guess it? How could she not see it? What she had done to him?

Hilal felt completely exposed.

He had noticed that Dunya looked at him with a certain kind of wonder too, but might it not be that this is how she looked at everyone? Was this not how a professional artist looked at anything and everything? And so it was very possible, and more than likely, that when she looked at him, what seemed to him like a look of love was nothing more than a look that a photographer would use to examine and assess and frame the object of his photograph. To all intents and purposes, he was nothing more to Dunya than a new and unique symmetry of light and darkness.

But instead of confessing to Dunya the truth about how he felt, or saying anything about the photograph she gave him (which already provided her with far too much incriminating evidence), Hilal slowly sipped from his yellow porcelain cup of tea.

"Did you really want to know the time yesterday?" Dunya asked him.

"No."

Dunya blushed and, without looking at him, added, "Because, you were wearing a watch."

Hilal wondered whether to run away, there and then. This was his one chance, his once-in-a-lifetime opportunity. She had taken hold of his heart without asking for permission, she had the power of life or death over it, she could hold it gently in her hands or toss it carelessly into a bin. Perhaps the wisest thing to do in the circumstances was to run, run, run. But instead he said to her, "If I try to kiss you will you slap me?"

"No," she said.

So this is how it happened. And most of it neither of them could remember clearly, nor understand. It was neither like this nor like that.

Love came to them like lightning, the way they'd both heard that it sometimes did.

Apart from his love for her (which was written all over his face), Dunya noticed something else in the first and second and all subsequent photographs she took of Hilal. It was clear and striking, like a line that divided his face in two parts. One

63

part was light and full of love and wonder and the other part was dark and full of something hidden. What was it, or who was it? What pain, what secret was Hilal hiding from her?

And as she thought about the mystery of Hilal, Dunya realized that it could only be one thing—a girl.

"Did a girl ever break your heart, Hilal?" she asked him.

"No. Never," he said.

"But I can see it in all the photographs I've taken of you, I can see clear signs of a heart that has been broken *in two*. Are you sure that a girl didn't do that to you? Are you sure there was never a girl you once loved in Aleppo and who did not love you back? I can almost see her; she's beautiful and bold. And if she were here she would cruelly take you away from me."

"No one can take me away from you. And least of all a girl who doesn't exist."

"Nor a boy?"

"A boy? Of course not a boy. No, I've never fallen in love with a girl, nor did a boy break my heart with his little hammer," Hilal said.

"But why this look in your eyes, and in your face?"

"What look?"

"A broken look . . . a lost look, it is as if you lost something and you haven't been able to forget it."

"I promise you Dunya, I have never had the honor before of having my heart broken by anyone, and neither have I suffered any great loss. I promise you, that you are imagining it. Only you can break my heart. My heart is in your hands," Hilal smiled.

"Then what is it, *who is it*?"

"It isn't anyone," Hilal said.

She could see the thing in him that he was hiding even from himself. And this was why he loved her.

Dunya focused her camera on Hilal's face and began to frame his profile against the horizon in the distance. Was he the boy she'd dreamed about all those years ago after she had discovered that love existed and begun to look for it in everyone's eyes?

Yes, it was him! Of course it was him and it could never be anyone except for him.

When she looked at him through her lens, she noticed that he was looking elsewhere. That was how it was, being with him. Sometimes even while he was sitting right next to her in the same room, on the same table, lying in the same bed, holding her in his arms, he would disappear, pieces of him would go missing, for hours and sometimes for days. And when she asked him where he had disappeared to he would never be able tell to her, because he didn't know.

Dunya had read that the moon had fourteen lunations, which is how she described the dance of light and darkness on Hilal's face.

10

Can Photography Tell the Truth?

IN THE SPRING OF 1994, two years after Hilal started secretly living with Dunya without the knowledge of his or her parents, Mr. and Mrs. Shihab received a parcel from their son. Inside it they found a photograph of him in which he looked happier than they had ever seen him. But there was something much deeper than happiness in his eyes and in his expression; their son now looked like a man who had finally found what he had been looking for. This was the look Suad had seen in her husband's eyes when he met her and had not left him since. It was then that Suad became sure that her son had fallen in love. Of course, she also knew that he would never tell her and that she would not dare to ask him, but the photograph said everything to her that she needed to know.

Together with the beautiful black-and-white photograph Hilal had sent to his parents as a gift, he had also packed a Polaroid camera with handwritten instructions on how to use it and a note asking them to take photos of themselves and send them back to him. He had realized that letters and telephone calls were not enough to communicate with people who were afraid of words.

Photographs began to arrive in small dusty envelopes plastered with President Hafez al-Assad stamps.

The first envelope that arrived contained a photograph of Suad and Said pretending to be happy, both dressed in black, she in a conservative high-necked dress and he in a suit. They'd obviously dressed up and put on artificially happy faces just for the photograph.

Hilal's father Said was a handsome, sensitive-looking man. He was too busy sewing to write long letters to his son, but he tried to write at least one short letter a month. Suad had never learned to read or write because her parents thought that these skills would not be needed in the kitchen or in the bedroom.

Sometimes Said and Suad went to the post office together and rang their son for only a minute or two, because a minute on the phone to England cost twenty-five lira, which was the price of twenty-five kilograms of bread. And so Hilal would call them back and they'd continue to talk, or mumble, about nothing in particular. "Do you have warm socks, darling? Does the bread taste good in England? Do you want us to send you food? Can you really speak English, like the English do? Oh, how clever you are."

The next month a photograph arrived of Hilal's bed and of his desk and favorite armchair. His father wrote underneath it, "When will you come to see us?" Then a photograph arrived of a cherry tree that grew in the courtyard. "Look how much Suha has grown."

"Who is Suha?" Dunya looked at the photograph closely. "I can't see anyone in this photograph."

"Suha is our cherry tree. My mother has a shrub in the kitchen that she calls Mahmoud and a cactus in the lounge that she calls Majid. Those are the names of her brothers whom she hasn't seen in years. I don't know who Suha is. It's the name of a beautiful faraway star that can't be seen with human eyes."

Dunya and Hilal's flat (not far from the Royal Observatory in Greenwich) filled with Polaroid photographs of Hilal's house in Syria, until Dunya began to imagine that she had been there many times. She saw his old-fashioned wooden bed, the round dining-room table, the kitchen, and the ancient-looking front door. Each photograph was posted separately with a letter written by his father telling him of things that were happening in the city: "The supply of butter is erratic. Toilet roll queues are getting longer. Thank God you are our only son and you don't have to serve in the army. Brothers are forced to kill brothers. I will say no more. Stay true to yourself, my son. Don't copy others and lose your true self. Remember each self is distinct and different."

Dunya and Hilal's flat was also filled with large photographs that Dunya had taken over the years. There was one of Hilal sitting on a chair looking out of the window, his face bright, while everything around him was hidden under a blanket of dark. In this photograph Hilal looked as if he were trying to say something really loudly but couldn't. What was he trying to say? Even he didn't seem to know.

One day the letters and photographs that Mr. and Mrs Shihab often sent in brown envelopes stopped coming. Their phone calls also came to an abrupt end and there were no replies to any of Hilal's letters.

After the fourth month of silence Hilal stopped counting, because he was buried in solving the most complex equation he had ever worked on and had almost reached the final stages of proving his theory of moonlight. Soon he would be ready to publish his first book: *Theories of the Effect of Moonlight on the Earth.*

"As soon as I send the manuscript off I'm going to Syria. Will you come with me, Dunya?" Hilal stood under some photographs that were drying on a line. "I want you to meet my parents."

"But I can't ever set foot in Syria again," Dunya said.

"Of course you can. It's been ten years since what happened with your teacher Miss Huda. You were a little girl then, now things are different. No one will remember what you did and what you said, and you have learned your lesson."

"What lesson is that, Hilal—to keep my mouth shut and do what I'm told or else go to prison or disappear? I don't know if I can ever learn a lesson like that."

"But this is the country you love, Dunya, you can't stay away for ever."

"Is it?" Tears ran down her cheeks.

"You need to go back, even if it's only once."

"Do I?"

"Only for two weeks. You will feel much better after that. You need to go back to feel complete." Hilal smiled. "And you must meet my parents."

"But you haven't even told them about me," Dunya said.

"I don't need to tell them anything, all they need is to *see* you with me, and me with you—and they'll understand everything. That's how we do things in our family."

"This wouldn't work with my father. If I turn up with you in Syria, he will go bananas. And I don't think I could take that, could you?"

"Are you sure?" Hilal said. "Why don't we try it? When your father sees how much I love you, I promise you he might even feel happy for us. In the abstract, on paper, yes, he will think this and that of me and you, but when he sees me with you and you with me, when he sees *our love*, he won't be able to argue with it. He won't have the heart to break something so perfect, so right, so meant to be."

"My father's not like yours. And I don't know if you're strong enough to handle him."

"I'm not strong enough? Is that so, Dunya? So why do you love me, then? I thought women only loved strong and powerful men?"

Dunya sat on Hilal's lap and began to inspect him as if to look for reasons, or excuses, which might justify her love for him. She cupped his face with both of her hands and examined different parts of it: "I love you because you're so handsome, perhaps that is the reason. I don't think I've ever seen a man as beautiful as you. I love you, not just because you are handsome, but perhaps because I simply cannot stop looking at you, a light seems to shine constantly in your face, which I cannot keep my eyes away from. I think that is why I love you. Or maybe it is because you're like the moon, and who can resist the moon? Every time I look at you I see something new, a different aspect, a previously hidden part. Maybe that's why. I was always told that I was far too curious and that this was going to lead me to much trouble. Maybe I love you *because* you're hidden. I love you because parts of you appear gradually and then they disappear. You're like a story I can never finish reading."

"Hmmm." Hilal looked at Dunya with concentration. He took two of her curls and rolled them around his fingers and began to study her closely. "Well, I love you for the opposite reasons that you love me. I love you because you see and you let yourself be seen. Nothing in you is hidden. This is the most powerful and beautiful thing I've ever witnessed. You don't hide and you have nothing to hide. You're fearless. I love that. And I love your beautiful curls and your mouth and your eyes and your cheeks and your . . . your body, *your body*." He lifted her up in the air. "I love your beautiful, graceful body. Is that a crime? I love you because I want you. It has to be you. It can't be any other."

Hilal placed Dunya on the floor and put his arms around her waist. "The only thing you hide from others, however, is me. Why can't you tell your father that you love me?"

Two days later a letter arrived from Syria, typed by a professional letter-typist. Some of the typewriter ink was diluted. Perhaps a glass of water had been spilled on the letter or maybe it had been raining while the letter-writer was typing it outside in the square. It was impossible to read many words or sentences in it, except for the following ones: "Six months ago . . . I could not tell you . . . Your father . . ."

And a line at the end: "Your father went to heaven, my son."

11

The Men Who Wear the Trousers

DUNYA HELD HER CAMERA CLOSE to her chest while a man with a pointed gray and black mustache and stripy trousers interrogated her. "Why do you have such a big camera? It doesn't look like a tourist's camera. Are you a spy?"

"Of course I'm not a spy. I'm a photographer," she answered.

"A what?"

"A photographer."

"Is that a job?"

"Yes."

"So what do you intend to photograph in the Democratic Republic of Syria?"

"I don't know yet."

"You don't know *yet*? But your job is to take photographs, isn't it? And you get paid to do that?"

"Yes."

"Photographs of things you don't know *yet*?"

"Exactly."

"And who tells you what photographs to take and why do they pay you for taking them? Were you given a list by the British Intelligence Services? You are a spy!"

"I promise you, Sir, that I am *not*. I take photographs of interesting-looking people mostly, doing interesting things and then I submit them to art competitions or galleries. Perhaps I can take a photograph of you?" Dunya took her camera lens cover off. "Spies don't use these types of cameras, look. This is too old-fashioned and only used for art photography. Spies hide their cameras in fountain pens and umbrellas, didn't you know? They don't work in the open like me. Do you mind if I take a photo of you?" she smiled at him.

The customs official became silent for a moment.

"I need to report this." The words traveled from between his teeth, crawled outside the boundaries of his oily mustache, and landed in Dunya's ear like a toothpick. He knitted his brows furiously, as if there was certain trouble in store for her, and walked off to a cubicle nearby.

"You shouldn't have told him you're a photographer. He doesn't know what it means and he'll spend hours making our life hell, particularly if he discovers that a girl like you makes a living by taking photos of things that mean nothing to him. Oh Dunya, Dunya, when will you learn?"

Hilal understood the psyche of these so-called 'officials.' He thought of them as lost souls who had nothing better to do or look forward to than what they were already doing. Instead of stamping people's passports, they seemed to be on a bitter revenge mission to stamp on as many travelers' egos as possible. They were particularly awful to Syrians who had been on foreign travels. They felt that the world was divided between people who traveled abroad and people who couldn't and that it was their patriotic duty to teach the former a lesson. The 'officials' seemed (and were) far more interested in sipping their sugared teas and walking as slowly as possible, especially when the queues were long or if the airplane had arrived after midnight (like now), than in doing their jobs. Instead of walking briskly to get from one office to another to clear a passport, they walked lazily, wearing traditional leather slippers—known as sharoukhs— and looking superior and contemptuous of everyone who wasn't one of them.

A middle-aged man, who looked slightly more senior than the first one, began to open Dunya's suitcase. "She doesn't look like a spy," he said to his subordinate. "Spies look nothing like *her*. Let me deal with her." He looked at Dunya with feigned tenderness. "Where did you come from?"

"London," she answered.

The middle-aged man looked at her with anticipation now. "Did you get me a present?" he whispered. Then he flipped a cigarette out of a box and put it in his mouth.

"No. I don't even know you, Sir," Dunya said innocently. The official winced with disappointment.

"But what about that lovely watch you're wearing. Didn't you bring this for me?" he said in a slightly menacing tone, pulling out a pink plastic lighter.

"But it's a girl's watch!" Dunya said, starting to understand what he was trying to tell her.

"My daughter would love it." Dunya unfastened her watch and looked at him as he gleefully closed her suitcase and let her go in peace, with her camera dangling safely from her shoulder.

Meanwhile Hilal was occupied elsewhere, talking to an official who had decided to stop him when he saw him holding his suspiciously large telescope. The official first thought the telescope was a machine gun or a rocket launcher, but once he believed that it was a machine with which one looked at the moon and other planets things got worse. He tried to convince Hilal that the telescope would make an ideal 'present' to him.

Finally Hilal said, "I'd have loved to give it to you, Sir, but unfortunately Mr. Hafez al-Assad would be disappointed as I've brought it especially for his son Bashar. He ordered it to be personally delivered from London by me!"

After hearing that, the official evaporated like dew at the touch of sunshine.

*

As Dunya and Hilal walked hand in hand toward the taxi rank at Damascus Airport, Hilal decided that he didn't want to go to Aleppo just yet. "I'm not ready to see my mother, not tonight, not tomorrow, nor the day after. I need to collect my thoughts before I see her. I don't want to cry in front of her; I don't want to be angry with her. I want to be a good son," he said to Dunya. "Why don't we go to Latakia to see your mother and father first?"

"But she's been waiting for you, Hilal, for six months!"

"No, no," Hilal said. "She hasn't been waiting for me for six months; she waited six months before she told me that my father was gone. What mother does that to her son?" Hilal's tears ran down his face. "I couldn't even say goodbye to him."

Their yellow, old-fashioned taxi (which looked as if it was held together with nothing more than sticky tape and perhaps a few squirts of industrial glue) drove into the city of Latakia early the next morning. From its half-broken windows, Dunya and Hilal watched the sun rising over the bright blue Mediterranean sea, bringing with it a blanket of humidity that covered them. Dunya lay her head on Hilal's chest as the taxi turned from street to street and she listened to his heartbeats.

He and she here in Latakia; his heart under her cheek.

The streets outside were still empty, but morning calls to prayer (mostly sung by tape recorders) were already booming through the air, echoed by other calls carried by deeper and weaker and sometimes comical voices, which repeated the same immortal words, again and again: *I profess that God is the Greatest and that Muhammad is the Messenger of God!*

And after that, they heard the ringing of church bells from the north and south and east and west of the city, which rang as if to say, "Good morning, good morning, to a new day."

"What a city! An entire city kissed by the sea, caressed by the wind, and protected by all these proud mountains and nourished by all these rich and fertile fields," Hilal exclaimed. "I've never seen this part of Syria."

Dunya felt the uncanny feeling that most people feel after a long separation from someone deeply beloved, and she was far too happy to speak. Like everyone else who had the fortune or misfortune of being born in this precious stretch of land and near this particular swathe of sea, Dunya was and always would be umbilically and emotionally attached to it.

The sun rose up in the sky bringing with it a heavy heat that Dunya had almost completely forgotten existed; a dreamy, enveloping heat that held her inside like a mother gathering a long lost daughter in her warm embrace.

A fleet of yellow taxis (most of them looking as if they certainly would be retired or fail their road safety inspections in more sensible countries) moved through the streets, hungry for lira, almost breaking down under the weight of the plastic flowers that adorned them; cars hooted like sick owls and trucks heaved, burdened with their loads of flour, melons, and live meadow cows. Most of these vehicles were inevitably adorned with plastic, glass, and feather accesories, complete with self-congratulatory, flirtatious, or provocative proclamations: "I'm as pretty as they come"; "Your eyes are my ocean"; "To hell with those who envy me!"

Now that they were nearer to the center, their taxi crossed through the old Latakia vegetable market, where at this time of day, it was like a festival. The biggest recompense for not being able to speak freely in the Republic of Syria was the freedom to sing and shout, and this is what all the vegetable and street sellers in Latakia, and all across the country, did in the mornings. Dunya watched, with awe and wonder, men of all ages, shapes, and sizes praising and extolling their produce louder and louder, like a chorus in an outdoor choir. A man emptied two large bags of apples on a table. Another one drove in with a blue truck packed full of red grapes, another truck came in loaded with fresh green figs. Hundreds of different men in all modes of transport—vehicle, animal, or on foot—had settled down for a day of trading mushrooms, lentils, melons, green beans, potatoes, tomatoes, items of clothing, electrical goods, knickknacks, and flowers. Each one shouted out the name of what they were selling, loudly and as if they were singing. Dunya's heart was filled with joy as she heard these familiar orchestras of men and boys singing competitively about their fruits and vegetables and rhythmically boasting about their products and wares:

Eggplant! Bananas, alfalfa sprouts!
Electric dice, radios, Chinese mice!
Talking birds, mints, and herbs, the best and shiniest price,
Spoil your wife, brighten her life, with perfumes and spice!

She lay her head on Hilal's chest and folded her arms around him. How would she have guessed ten years ago that she would be returning here with her One True Love, both delivered in a yellow taxi to her door? She smiled.

And as the taxi dropped them on the corner of Baghdad Street, a few steps away from the building where Mr. and Mrs. Noor lived, Dunya stood outside and took a deep breath.

Now that her feet were standing on Latakia's dusty ground, that her eyes were filled with the color of its electric-blue sky, which seemed to be everywhere all at once, she could no longer deny it: she was home at last! Everywhere she and Hilal looked they could hear Arabic, Arabic, Arabic. Everywhere they turned they saw children playing in the streets, widows wearing black, and men playing backgammon on balconies and in cafés, slowly sipping their cups of coffee as if there was nothing to worry about except for deciphering the meaning of the sky that day, and tasting the flavors of the day. Arabic, Arabic, Arabic, its heart-expanding words and sounds and intonations, words they had not heard for so long and which pointed to and described feelings and states of being and seeing that they had forgotten existed. Dunya had also forgotten about the air, Latakia's air. And as she breathed it in, tears fell upon her cheeks. Latakia with all its imperfections and flaws was not an ordinary city to her, it was more like a mother or a father or a beloved grandmother; it was her tree and she was its branch.

12

Joseph's Heart

WHEN JOSEPH NOOR OPENED HIS front door that morning, he didn't see what he was expecting to see. It was not the corner shop delivery boy or the plumber he'd rung for earlier. Instead he saw his daughter Dunya looking at him with her big green eyes—and next to her stood a tall young man with disheveled curly hair carrying what appeared to be her suitcase.

"But I thought you weren't arriving until the day after tomorrow my darling girl! Why come on your own in a taxi, when I could've picked you up?" Joseph put his arms around Dunya and pressed her to him and made loud kissing noises. "These independent English habits you have picked up are so unsuitable for a girl. What are dads for, if daughters don't need them?" He squeezed her cheek as if she were still a little girl. "You can leave her suitcase here young man." Joseph pulled some notes out of his pocket and handed them to Hilal.

"Dad, this is Hilal," Dunya said.

"Hilal?" Joseph stared at Hilal for a moment or two as if he were trying to remember that name and who the person it belonged to was. Suddenly a light bulb lit up in his head. "Hilal! No, no, no. Please don't tell me it's him. *No!* Absolutely not!"

Joseph pulled Dunya by her arm and appeared to be trying to shut the front door in Hilal's face.

"Dad! I want you to talk to Hilal, I want you to meet him. He wants to meet you. You *must* talk to him, Dad."

"You brought *him* all the way from London to talk to *me*, even though you knew how much I don't want to talk to him, nor see his face, nor hear his name?" he said. "And you say that I must . . . *I must?* Who's the dad here?"

"I thought that if . . ."

"If? If what?" Joseph said in a bitter, whistle-like voice. "Dunya, Dunya. You are so . . . so, so, *so* . . ." he kept repeating the word *so* as if his tongue was stuck—"so shameless!" Joseph finally said it. "Yes. Shameless! Shameless!"

Dunya took one of Hilal's hands in hers.

"Dr. Noor, I was the one who insisted that Dunya bring me to see you, despite . . ." Hilal began.

"Despite?" Joseph looked at Hilal with disdain. "Despite, huh? Despite what?"

Dunya looked at Joseph and saw that his face was turning white now, then it seemed to be transforming itself into a strange shade of green, and then a sort of eerie blue hue began to envelop it. "Dad? Are you alright, Dad?" Dunya put her arms around Joseph again, "Don't have a heart attack, Dad. I don't want you to die!"

"Die?" Joseph looked at Hilal with cold anger. "If you don't want me to die, don't marry him, it's very simple."

Dunya held her father's hands in hers, "Dad, Hilal and I love one another, but we're not in a hurry to get married. Talk to him a little, please, Dad. There's no harm in you talking to him, is there? Why can't you invite him for a cup of coffee? I know Mum wants to meet him."

"He loves you but has no plans to marry you? Now that sounds like a perfectly decent young man to me, with perfectly honest intentions. Oh, I feel so very comforted to hear that!" Joseph wished he could punch Hilal in the teeth and be done with him. *What is it with these upstart young men?* he wondered. But then it occurred to him that the neighbors next door might be eavesdropping and there was no way he wanted them to bear witness to this conversation.

*

"Patricia! Your daughter's here," Joseph called up the staircase, before ushering Dunya and Hilal into his chandeliered lounge.

Hilal had never been in a house like this before nor met a man like Joseph. No one with that degree of snobbery and sense of entitlement circulated in his parents' lives, nor in the corridors and lecture halls of Aleppo University. Who did he think he was? King of Syria? Yes, Joseph certainly behaved like a king, or a feudal lord, his home certainly looked like a palace, but he was only human, and no one was better than anyone else. A few thousand pieces of stone cemented together to make a beautiful house, more money in the bank, a family bloodline to boast of, a foreign education, all these things were not enough to make one person worth more than another in Hilal's eyes.

Soon a tall, glamorous English woman arrived in a cloud of perfume. She looked like a movie star with her perfectly made-up face and exquisitely tailored dress, her manicured nails, and perfect eyelashes. Patricia was exactly as Dunya had described her to him, in every detail, and she and Joseph looked like such an unlikely but inevitable couple—like black and white, like day and night.

"Dunya!" Patricia said. "Oh, darling child!" She ran toward her daughter and embraced her while looking over her shoulders at Hilal.

Unfortunately, even though Patricia tried not to, she couldn't contain herself and she involuntarily fluttered her eyeslashes at Hilal. He was so handsome! Much more so in the flesh than in the photograph she had seen of him. Patricia's instant and visible liking for Hilal made Joseph wish he could throw him out of the window then and there. But when he had another closer look at Hilal he realized how much taller than him he was, and how much stronger, and how much younger and how much . . . better looking. And the fact that Patricia saw it too was truly the last straw for Joseph.

Uh-oh. Patricia thought to herself when she saw her husband's face.

Hilal wore light blue trousers and a simple white shirt. Dunya stood next to him and continued to hold one of his hands.

Simply by looking at him, and sensing his presence and personality, Patricia could see that Hilal was indisputably tailormade for Dunya. It wasn't just physical, but also metaphysical. And their love was clear (for anyone with eyes) to see, but she knew that these indisputable signs of Love wouldn't be enough for Joseph. *Why did Dunya's love have to come in the shape of a boy so totally unsuitable? I mean, what man worth his salt could bear to see their daughter married to a man of such lowly origins, and with such long hair?*

Hilal's pitch-black curly hair flew up into the air in a poetic and rather touching way, like Dunya's (but with an added unexpected flourish). Yes, his hair was slightly too long for a man and a little untidy perhaps, but it suited him perfectly and gave him a cheeky and romantic character. He had overgrown stubble and was a little scruffy, but that was completely eclipsed and compensated for by his disarming smile and the gentle aura of innocence that surrounded him like scent.

"Good to meet you, Mrs. Noor, I've heard so much about you," Hilal said to Patricia with his deep and beautiful voice.

"Good to meet you too, Hilal," Patricia said and shook his hand.

Joseph could not contain his irritation any longer.

"Why?" he declared. "Why are we all standing here together like this, as if this is normal and acceptable? We don't live in London, Mr. Shihab, do we? Nor in Honolulu. We live in Syria, and here in Syria a girl is not allowed to have a boyfriend. She can be officially engaged to a man, but only with her father's permission, it's not up to her to decide. Do you have my permission, Mr. Shihab, to consort and cohort with my daughter Dunya? Did I give it to you? No. And so you have no place here in our house, or holding my daughter's hand in front of me. What she does behind my back is one thing, but right here in front of me, in my house! What a cheek you both have. What a lack of manners and consideration!" Joseph looked bright yellow now. Patricia anxiously inspected him and began to fear for what might happen next. *Oh no.* She froze in terror.

"Mr. Noor, if you give me a chance, I could explain my feelings for Dunya to you. They are true and genuine. I understand what you say and your concerns. But couldn't you give me a chance to at least prove to you who I am and that my love for Dunya is real?"

"Why should I care if your love for my daughter is real or not? Who cares? It's the least of my problems and it doesn't worry me in the least. My problem and concern is that my daughter is not for the likes of you, Mr. Shihab. Why don't you go and find yourself a girl of your own station? This is what I don't understand," Joseph said. "A plumber's daughter, perhaps? A mechanic's niece, a baker's sister! I don't care. Just not *my* daughter!"

Hilal looked at Joseph patiently, as if he was hoping for the storm to pass. He looked at Dunya and she looked at him as if that is what they'd expected and this is how they'd agreed to react.

"Joseph!" Patricia said. "Please excuse my husband, Hilal," she said. "He doesn't mean what he said. Let's have some tea. Amina!" Patricia called her maid who suddenly appeared as if out of nowhere, "My dear, could you make us tea and bring some biscuits?"

"Tea and biscuits?" Joseph said. "This is certainly not an occasion for tea and biscuits!"

Soon, soon he will change his mind, Hilal reassured himself, *when he sees how much I love her.*

"Dr. Noor," Hilal said with a strong but gentle voice, "I know you want a good husband for your daughter. I know you think that I'm not good enough for her. But I love her,

Dr. Noor, and she loves me, and it's not you or I or she who can make such decisions or choose the person we can or cannot love, it's our hearts that decide. I promise you, Dr. Noor, that I will make Dunya happy. Don't you want your daughter to be happy?"

Joseph glared at Dunya and then at Hilal, "Happy?"

"Yes, Dad, no other man could make me happy except for Hilal, he's the only One. Can't you see it?"

"The only One?" Joseph said with incredulity. "As it happens, no, I don't see it! What I can see, however, as brightly as the sun is that you two are pathologically naive and idealistic and that your idealism and naiveté are dangerous! You're deluded and completely out of your minds! And furthermore, you have no manners whatsoever. How, how—could you turn up like this uninvited, knowing that I didn't want to see you, Mr. Shihab?"

"Dr. Noor, I thought that . . . well, that—well, I felt that I had no other choice."

"Dad, can't you see how much I love Hilal and how much he loves me? Can't you see our love? And can't you see that Hilal isn't the wolf that you think he is?"

"A wolf? Oh no, he's certainly no wolf, he is far, far worse than that, he's a sheep! And I'm not having my daughter marrying a sheep. Look at his hair!" Joseph pointed at Hilal's wild black curls. "A black sheep!"

Joseph tried to pull Dunya away from Hilal by the arm, but Dunya held Hilal's arm tighter.

"If you decide to make a spectacle of yourselves and make sure everyone in this city hears of your and Hilal's *love* for one another, you will be ruined, do you hear me? Not only will you be ruined, but you will ruin our family's name! We will all be spectacularly ruined! Promise me you will keep Hilal a secret, promise!" Joseph said.

"Why should I hide him, Dad? I love him and he loves me."

"Because in this city, in this country, in this house the art of keeping secrets is an essential survival tool and a highly prized social skill. The price of failing to suppress the truth is very high, my dear, *anything*—from social ostracism to prison. Are you prepared to pay this price, Dunya? Well, even if you are, I am not."

Joseph stood up and continued: "I'm not against love per se, Dunya, if that is what you think. What you don't seem to understand is that this type of young man, a man of Hilal's type. . . . If you knew his type, you wouldn't be so starry-eyed about him. There are so many stars in your eyes, that what you see is not *him*, you're blind. But I'm your father and I can *see*, I can see the truth.

"*Either*," he turned to Hilal, "either you go home to Aleppo of your own free will within the hour, and leave my daughter alone and have nothing to do with her ever again—*or else*." Joseph waved his index finger in the air as if he had the power to cause terrible things to happen.

Then he walked out of the lounge and slammed the door loudly behind him.

Tea and biscuits soon arrived and Patricia went to sit on the sofa next to Dunya and held her in her arms. "Oh Dunya, Dunya, you haven't changed one bit. Not one bit. You still don't understand, not even the *basics*. You don't even possess a basic working knowledge." Patricia looked at her daughter with mounting anxiety. Ten years in England had not changed her one bit. It was probably the worst place for a girl like her, where eccentricity and freedom of speech were all the rage. There was trouble ahead. Yes, trouble ahead—Patricia could see it clearly, as if she were a psychic.

"You should learn to conduct your affairs discreetly, darling," Patricia said to Dunya while looking at Hilal in an ambiguous way.

"But Hilal is not an affair," Dunya said, "I'll never give him up."

"You want to kill your father and you want to turn me into a widow, is that it?"

"Of course I don't want you to turn into a widow, nor kill my father," Dunya said.

"Well then," Patricia continued on unabated. "Then you must try and be sensible, and Hilal, my son, you must try to encourage Dunya to *at least* pretend she's a good daughter while you're in Latakia. Don't destroy everything your father has worked for, his name and his reputation, Dunya! Try to understand how he feels. And try also, for a moment, to think how awful it would be for me to live as a lonely widow in this city! Put yourself in my shoes for once, Dunya."

"You'll never become a widow, Mama. Dad will not die just because I introduced him to Hilal."

"Won't he?" Patricia averted her gaze from her daughter in a bid to increase Dunya's sense of guilt and daughterly compassion.

Dunya took a sip of her tea and a bite from her biscuit and then went upstairs to find Joseph.

"So is it true you're an astronaut?" Patricia asked Hilal while he tried to sip his tea.

"Astronomer, you mean?"

"Oh yes, so you look at the stars do you?" Patricia blushed.

"I do sometimes look at the stars, but mostly at the moon. I'm a moonlight specialist. I study the effect of moonlight on our planet."

Although Hilal said this in a matter-of-fact way, Patricia was now really worried: what would Joseph think of him if he heard all this nonsense? Patricia realized that things could only get worse if he agreed to talk to Hilal. Joseph hated men who were too poetic, or radical in their thinking. He loved the down-to-earth, old-fashioned variety who could always be relied on to toe the line and do what they were told. Unlike Dunya and Hilal, who anyone could see were masters of the unexpected and the bold, and stubbornly refused to fit into any mold.

People like Hilal who didn't know their place and always wanted to be different, were a thorn in Joseph's side, and being with a man like that would only exacerbate Dunya's lack of realism, and would expose her to mortal danger were she to spend any length of time in Syria. But before making up her mind about Hilal, once and for all, Patricia decided to subject him to a little test.

"I think you're a wonderful man, Hilal," she said. "And I can perfectly understand why Dunya loves you. But I must warn you about Dunya. She's my only daughter, after all— and of course I love her dearly. But she has a flaw, Hilal, which you must be aware of."

"What flaw, Mrs. Noor?"

"Well . . ." Patricia hesitated a little before spilling the beans. "I don't know how quite to put it to you Hilal, you must've noticed it yourself."

"No, I haven't, what is it?" Hilal asked.

"Well, many years ago Dunya gave her heart to the art of photography. And a girl like that is not the sort of girl most men would consider to be a good future wife. She is different from the usual girls a mother might be looking for for her son. And if you are serious about her, you must take that into consideration and be able to accept it and live with it. She is not going to be a *wife*, if that is what you're expecting her to be one day."

"But how can that be a flaw, Mrs. Noor? That is precisely why I like her. That's what I love about her."

"You're still young and you don't understand these things, my son. A girl who gives her heart to art is a girl who doesn't have a heart. It's self-evident. To all intents and purposes you might be nothing more to her than an idea, or at best a dream. Real love between men and women is about much more than what you and Dunya think it is. Love is not just a series of loud

89

heartbeats followed by passionate kissing, nor is it to be found in the exploding sound of thunder and lightning. Love happens after that, when the fireworks are over, when the lights are off, it happens in the dark—that is when you see clearest. When I was young . . . I was delusional too, like you two, and look what happened to me." Patricia sipped the last bit of her cold tea and then stopped talking, because she could see that Hilal was not listening to her. But in his eyes she saw what she thought was the twinkle of tears.

"I was very sorry to hear about your father, Hilal. If there's any way I can be of help, please let me know. You seem like such a sensitive man." She took a handkerchief out of her handbag and gave it to Hilal, for she hoped that he'd start crying, and perhaps then she could put her arms around him to console him.

What a good-looking and charming son-in-law he would have been in another country, or at another time.

13

God the Father

THE GOD DISORDER AFFLICTED SYRIAN fathers in the main—not only Joseph. It struck as predictably as a major type of flu might, a couple of years after a Syrian man's wife turned into a mother by giving birth to at least one child (a son preferably). The father in question would often start to show symptoms of the disorder as soon as his child(ren) began to display any signs of independent thought or action. Soon enough, the tendency would develop into a full-blown condition where the father in question would become convinced that the proper powers and functions of fathers in a family setting should mirror the powers and functions of God (Version 0.1, Old Testament) with regard to humanity. This implied that their paternal powers included: Judgment, Punishment, Reward, as well as supernatural powers such as Seeing Into the Future (aka Prophecy).

"Listen, Dunya," Joseph said the following morning. "I have decided to give you my blessing to go and visit Hilal at his hotel. Why don't you go and have lunch with him and then invite him over here for dinner. I think I might be ready to talk to him. If it's true that he's as wonderful as you and your mother think he is, then perhaps, if you really love him, well, then perhaps I will try to be nice to him. I'm not as hard-hearted as you two think." Joseph looked at Patricia as if to check whether she was suitably impressed. "There's no harm in giving a poor young man a chance, is there?"

"Are you sure, Dad? Oh, Dad!" Dunya went to Joseph and put both her arms around his belly until she nearly suffocated him.

"I'm not as evil as you thought I was, darling, am I?" Joseph said.

"I never thought you were, Dad," Dunya smiled.

"But nevertheless, try to keep a low profile, don't forget where we are—that this is not Honolulu."

Dunya couldn't believe her ears. Perhaps Hilal was right after all and her father could be open to persuasion.

Hotel Bride of the Sea was a small two-star hotel perched on the Latakia seafront. It had once been painted yellow, in 1943, and had long, green, French-style wooden shutters, which let in sunlight and moonlight in equal measure but hid hotel customers from the excessively nosy gaze of passersby. Its balcony had unbroken views of the Mediterranean and its long horizon, which was drawn like a line that divided each day from the next like pages in a book.

As Dunya approached the front of Hotel Bride of the Sea, a 1950s blue Buick taxi stopped next to her and a young woman wearing a pair of high-heeled, pistachio-colored sandals stepped out of it and waved at her.

Who is she? Dunya wondered to herself.

The young woman's brown locks glistened in the sunlight, and as she came nearer to Dunya, Dunya saw her familiar, beautiful, almond-shaped, olive-green eyes, but she still did not know who she was. The young woman began to call out her name: "Dunya, Dunya! Oh my God. Ya Allah, *Dunya, Dunya,* my darling, habibti!" She put her arms around her and smudged her cheeks with her red lipstick and looked at her with utter delight.

The young woman's eyelashes were so long and undulating that they almost looked artificial.

"Excuse me, but—who are you?" Dunya asked her politely as she extricated herself out of her arms. "How do you know my name?"

"Who am I?" the young woman said. "How do I know your name? Shame on you! Shame on you, Dunya! *I'm Maria.* Have you forgotten me?"

"Maria?" Dunya said. "But you look so different, so grown up! So made-up! I've never seen you like this!" Dunya put her arms around Maria again and kissed her on her cheeks. "Maria! Maria!"

"You haven't changed in the slightest! The same wild hair, the same dreamy eyes, everything the same! Why didn't you call me as soon as you arrived, you traitor? My dad told me you weren't coming until next week."

"It's a . . . long story."

"If there's a story, I must be the first to hear it. Tell me."

"Strictly speaking, it must be kept a secret. Can you keep a secret?" Dunya took Maria's hand in hers and they walked toward the entrance of Hotel Bride of the Sea.

"What a question?" Maria said. "I could teach a degree-level course in the art of keeping secrets," Maria said.

"Well in that case, come with me, my secret spent the night in this hotel. Do you want to meet him?" Dunya pointed at the hotel.

"Your secret is *a man?*"

"He certainly is," Dunya said.

"What sort of a man?" Maria looked at the hotel with suspicious eyes. "What sort of man stays in a hotel like this?" Maria looked at the shabby entrance. No self-respecting Latakian or any of their guests would be seen dead in a hotel like this—exclusively frequented by lowlifes, shopkeepers, truckers, and disreputable types.

"The man I love."

"*Oh,*" Maria answered. "In that case I must meet him. Did you bring him with you from London? Is he English?"

"Hilal's originally from Aleppo."

"Hilal? From Aleppo?" Maria was taken aback. "I see. How do your father and mother feel about this?"

"They both like him."

"Your father likes him?" Maria said incredulously. "That Joseph is full of surprises, I must say. My father would've killed me if I brought home a man like that. I never heard of such a thing. Hilal must be an exceptionally charming young man to be able to have that effect on your father, despite all the other qualities he possesses, such as his name. With a name like that he must surely be a low-class Muslim boy, right? How did you manage that, all the way in London? We all thought you'd come back with an English lord or someone impressive like that."

Maria decided to risk her carefully guarded reputation and step inside the disreputable Hotel Bride of the Sea in order to get a sneak preview of Hilal. Of course, she was going to do it discreetly and not mention it to anyone afterward.

The possession of a secret or two was a necessity for any prim and proper girl with a reputation to uphold in Latakia. But Maria was neither as prim as she pretended to be, nor as proper. Some hardened Latakian gossips had even decided that she was a bit of a *rebel* because she sometimes smoked while she walked and on occasion had been spotted eating a sandwich on her way home. Eating sandwiches in public was considered vulgar and very unbecoming for a girl like Maria. Some people even thought that she was presumptuous because she'd entered the Miss Latakia Beauty Competition, and that she was vain and probably had corrupt contacts because she'd won it. Girls were both happy and unhappy because she wasn't married yet. And before her recent highly publicized engagement to Shadi, many young women had been worried sick that she would steal their future husbands and that eligible men might ask for her hand—rather than theirs. It was preposterous. Her hand was in demand. And her prize of twenty pairs of Yves St. Laurent shoes, specially flown in from Paris, was the most irritating thing of all. Her designer-clad feet were now in demand too.

As she stood inside Hotel Bride of the Sea's main reception, next to Dunya, Maria half-closed her eyes like a little girl who hopes that if she can't see what she's doing then others won't be able to see it either. "If someone sees us walking into such a trashy hotel," she whispered in Dunya's ear, "we'll be *finished*."

The hotel receptionist Abu Zahra was busy filing his nails at the desk. He looked at Dunya and then at Maria and wondered whether they were a new type of traveling hooker. And if they were, would it not be bad for the reputation of the hotel, whose clientele included a prominent array of single men and sometimes families with high moral standards? This was a good quality hotel. He wanted to keep it that way. He twisted the tips of his mustache. It was the sort of hotel where prominent shopkeepers came in the afternoons to discuss business over a hookah pipe. One didn't want their wives to get worried.

"What do you want? Don't you know that single girls in hotels ring alarm bells!" he announced theatrically. He then put his nail file away and pulled out some worry beads out of his trouser pocket.

"We're here to see Mr. Hilal Shihab," Dunya said. "Could you call him and tell him that Miss Dunya Noor is here?"

"I would if I could," the receptionist said, while grimly twisting the tip of his mustache with one hand while rolling his worry beads in the other.

"Well, why can't you?" Dunya asked.

"Because he's already gone."

"Gone where?" Dunya said.

"Gone with two men who took him off in a Mercedes with darkened windows. One of them carried his suitcase and the other one carried that large instrument he claims is a *telescope*! And off they went." The receptionist looked at Dunya with eyes as small and black as peppercorns.

"So what you're telling me is that he checked out?"

"Yes, exactly so." The receptionist coughed lightly, before producing a slim, green vegetable smile.

"A Mercedes with black windows?" Maria interrupted.

This was the sort of car unusually driven by members of the Hizb (the Baath Party) or the Mukhabarat (the secret service).

"Yes, exactly that sort of vehicle," the receptionist agreed. "He must be a young man with strong personal connections, a big wasta." He stared at Maria. *What eye makeup that young woman had.* It turned his head, slightly. *Makeup was made in the factories of Satan, the Lord of Darkness. And her perfume, well, these were the fumes of hell.*

"But Hilal doesn't have these sorts of connections. Could that car have been a taxi?" Dunya asked.

The receptionist took an al-Hamra cigarette out of his pocket, and lit it nervously. "Who am I to say?" he said.

"Well," Joseph said to Dunya, "If you knew the truth about men, Hilal's disappearance would make perfect sense to you. You girls are so naive, and so idealistic. The truth is, young men don't fall in love with one girl and one girl only, to them girls like you are like daisies in a field, they pick one and then another, and they soon tire of that one too. I was once like that," Joseph looked at Patricia, "before I met your mother."

"You really think that Hilal has run away?" Patricia said. "He seemed like such a decent young man, and I saw the love in his eyes—for Dunya, I saw it Joseph!"

"You didn't see anything, you imagined it," Joseph said in the voice of a world-weary expert in the cruel realities of men's fickle hearts. "Imagination is a dangerous faculty that Dunya's highly blessed with," Joseph addressed Patricia.

"Hilal loves me," Dunya said. "I know it for a fact. He would never run away from me like that and in such a cowardly way! Never, Dad. Something must've happened to him, or else it must be a misunderstanding. Did you ask him to leave for my sake? Or did you send those men from the Mukhabarat to take him home? Was it you, Dad?"

"Mukhabarat? What kind of man do you think I am, Dunya?" Joseph said with outrage. "What a way to speak to your father? The Mukhabarat have much more important things to do than give a wimp like Hilal a free ride home. No, this car sounds more like a luxury taxi staffed by two men, one to drive and one to carry the luggage. He probably wanted to make himself look like a big shot, they all like showing off when they come back home from abroad," Joseph said. "What delusions of grandeur. It's truly laughable."

"Hilal isn't a like that, he doesn't care about such things," Dunya said. "Something must've happened to him, something fishy, and I'm going to find out what it is."

Joseph sat on the sofa and rested both his arms on his paunch. "Amina! Amina, bring us lunch!" he said in a sonorous voice.

"I'm going to Aleppo, Dad, and I'm going to find Hilal and find out what happened to him. And if it turns out that it was you who told him to go, for my sake or something, if it's because of you that he left, then . . ."

"Then what?" Joseph asked lazily.

"Well, then I'll never come back to this country again. What kind of country is this? And what kind of father are you?" Dunya's tears began to fall. "No one's allowed to do anything, not even fall in love. Even love is a crime here."

"I promise you that Hilal did not leave Latakia because of me, and that there is nothing the matter with this country. At least we have customs and traditions. At least there is respect. Do you even understand the meaning of this word, Dunya? You're not going to Aleppo!"

"I'm going to Aleppo to find him," Dunya said. "Just try to stop me."

Joseph looked at his daughter with furrowed brows: *who did she inherit this stubborn streak from? She was insufferable!*

BOOK THREE
The Truth about Hilal

Truth is like a bird, difficult to capture,
Listen to her song and try to ask her:
"Who are you? Who are you?"
Ask her once, ask her twice,
Ask until you hear her voice!

14

The City of Boys

LIKE EVERY CITY IN SYRIA, Aleppo seemed to be heavily popu-
lated by men and boys. Almost everywhere Dunya looked she
saw boys, boys, boys. Boys who, regardless of whether they
were four, five, six, ten, eleven, twelve, or fourteen, behaved as
if they were big men with big wide shoulders, hungry mouths
to feed and households to run—as though they had better be
tough to cope. And it was clear from the proud expressions on
their faces that they were all fully aware of the importance of
their future destinies as *men*.

The men of Aleppo often called one another 'batal,' hero,
but many of them and particularly the shopkeepers and crafts-
men thought of themselves as kings: the King of Melons, the
King of Biscuits, the King of Cakes, the King of Cardamom,
the King of Perfumes, the King of Falafel, the King of Zucchini, the King of Soap—and finally Dunya found the King
of the World, who owned a shop that sold more than one
thing, including TVs, aerials, radios, and washing machines.

In the old town of Aleppo different historical eras were
mixed up haphazardly. Boys on donkeys and others on motorbikes passed Dunya by leisurely; soldiers proudly paraded
their Kalashnikovs on their shoulders while chewing gum and
eyeing up the women, as if this was their full-time job—even
more important than saving the country. Women wearing jeans
and fashionable skirts walked next to bearded men in turbans
and robes and women whose heads, faces, and bodies were

covered entirely in black polyester cloth. These veiled women walked everywhere, carrying shopping bags, their black shoes hiding their feet, their silence hiding their thoughts; looking like secrets that had come to life. Many of the young women of Aleppo walked as if trying to hide, as if by walking quietly and quickly from A to B no one would see them. Like this, no one could inspect them, quantify them, assess their worth; no one could say that they were trying to get attention or flaunting their wares.

Dunya asked some shopkeepers if they happened to know where the His & Hers Sewing Atelier was, or whether they'd heard of Hilal the Astronomer or his parents Tailor Said and Seamstress Suad, but they vehemently shook their heads.

"Could it not be that you have been misled?" the first one told her. "Perhaps they live in Damascus. We don't have young men who work as astronomers in this city. What a fanciful idea!"

"To tell you the truth, no girl should go in pursuit of a young man, even if he happens to be an astronomer, never, never!" another shopkeeper advised her. "Go back home, Mademoiselle, before your parents start worrying about you." He pointed an admonishing finger at her, and then continued to tout for more customers.

Finally Dunya sat down in a pastry shop and ordered a glass of tea, which a boy served to her on a small silver tray. She watched him from the corner of her eye as he went back to his little workstation in the back of the café where he was shoveling handfuls of almonds into little plastic bags. An old man who looked like his grandfather, perched on a wooden stool beside him and began to collect the bags in a cardboard box, while whistling a playful tune.

Dunya took her camera out and captured the boy and his grandfather—two men separated by a distance of only fifteen centimeters and seventy years of laughter and tears.

Soon after that, a boy dressed in a man's suit came and joined Dunya at her table. He had carefully combed hair, with a straight side-parting, and was holding a thick book of mathematics in one of his hands. "Hey lady, how about taking a picture of me?" he said, trying to make his soft boyish voice sound deeper than it was, "My name is Marwan." He shook his little shoulders proudly. Dunya imagined that this was what Hilal was like fifteen years ago. As she looked at the boy through her viewfinder, she imagined him pulling a cigarette out of his pocket and beginning to discuss his latest current affairs concerns. Perhaps he would discuss the Palestinian Question with her, or the distinctions between Socialism, Capitalism, and Communism. She wouldn't have been surprised, as this is what young boys were like in Syria. There were boys who were shopkeepers, boys who baked bread, and boys who were pastry chefs. She saw a boy who was a plumber, another who was a street-gang leader. One boy was a budding comedian, another one carried himself with the air of a street preacher. Some boys seemed like bosses and others like underlings.

As one boss-type of boy saw Dunya passing down an alley, he called out to his gang of friends who were blocking her passage, "Saliiiiim! Saliiiim! Jamal, Hakim, Fadi, Karim, c'mon, move out of the lady's way!" They all instantly obeyed.

"What are you doing in our city, Miss?" a boy asked her. "Where do you come from?"

"I'm looking for a young man by the name of Hilal Shihab, the son of Said and Suad the tailor and seamstress? Have you heard of him?" Dunya asked.

"Is he your sweetheart?" the boy replied.

"Yes," Dunya answered.

"And you say that his name is Hilal?"

"Yes," Dunya said.

"If he's like the moon, he'll turn up soon!" the boy sang out in a loud melodic voice, then ran off.

As it happened a crescent moon was due to appear that evening.

Dunya examined the endless number of birds that flew over her head from every direction, and noted how their songs (and even the flapping of their wings) could always be heard above the metallic sounds of hammers and cars and trucks and engines and machinery of every kind all over Aleppo. This wasn't a city only full of boys, it was also teeming with birds.

Aleppo's old town might be small in the eyes of many, but its alleys (if properly measured with a heavy duty measuring tape) were no shorter than twelve kilometers of imperfect circles and mind-boggling labyrinths. It was slowly dawning on Dunya that her attempt to find Hilal by asking a random sample of boys and shopkeepers whether they knew where he lived was a little unrealistic. Finding Hilal in the old town of Aleppo was beginning to seem like trying to find a needle in a haystack.

But Dunya was sure that she would find him—if not that night, then definitely the next morning if she turned up at the Aleppo University Physics Department, where one of the professors was bound to know him. Was he not their star student?

The sun was getting stronger and stronger and the city of Aleppo was getting hotter and hotter with the breath of passing donkeys acting as another rather unexpected source of heat. Numerous electric and manual fans cooled the old town's alleyways and shops, as most people couldn't afford air-conditioning, but there was some merciful protection between people and the sky in the form of paper bags, recycled trash bags, plastic sheets, and wooden planks, which were used as makeshift ceilings above the alleys.

Everything in this city filled Dunya's heart with a feeling she had long forgotten, a feeling of love toward everything around her. Yes, it was true that Syria was still living in the past, but perhaps it was this very forgetfulness of the present, this unhurried lack of self-consciousness, this strange un-modern innocence that was what she had missed so much. And every time she thought of Hilal, she wished that he was holding her hand and walking beside her, here in this beautiful old city where he was born.

Dunya took her camera out again and tried to take more photographs of every aspect of Aleppo and every one of its many faces. By contemplating each one of them and examining them separately, she was sure she might uncover the truth about Aleppo and what she imagined was its soul. For each city had a soul, each street a story and each face a secret mystery and a long and convoluted history.

She held her camera with both of her hands and began first by taking a photograph of Aleppo's light and the outline of its shadows. Inside these rays of black and white, Dunya thought she could see the shape of Hilal's face—as a little boy, and as a man, how he had been and how he was now and how he might one day become. She imagined his beautiful eyes appearing and disappearing into the stream of sunlight that filled the streets in startling bursts, like waves dashing themselves on a distant shore.

15

The Professor of Love

BECAUSE OF THE MALEVOLENT INFLUENCE of Hafez al-Assad
and his mustachioed band of Baathist young men, Syria had
become a pariah state of great renown. And so, even a city
with Aleppo's extraordinary charm, beauty, and history was
tainted by the *shame* of being the second largest in a thriv-
ing police state. Only Western secret agents, Russian and
East German engineers and military experts, and the most
intrepid of tourists dared set foot there. Well-to-do and fashion-conscious Syrians, on the other hand, were not in the least
impressed by the old city of Aleppo, mainly because it was not
like Paris, nor like London, and certainly *nothing* like Beirut.

But Dunya felt differently. She loved every speck of dust in
Aleppo, and every jasmine flower that grew on every Aleppan
jasmine tree. She felt love for its people, for its air, and for its
sky, and for every stone and every door and every house and
every window, and for all the faces which looked at and away
from her; each one of whom could've or might've been Hilal
or his mother, or his neighbor, teacher, or friend.

A moody but rather marvelous-looking horse was flip-
ping his hairy tail left and right, as he pulled a cart laden
with fresh plums through a narrow alley. Dunya focused her
camera on his large and proud face and included his neck-
lace of red and green beads in her shot. The horse yawned
and then spat on the floor as if he'd had enough. Enough,
enough, enough! After spitting for the fifth time, he stopped

trotting and began to stare at the window of a dessert shop next to him with wide-open eyes, ignoring his rider's angry whip. He inspected the shop window carefully, as if he were trying to decide whether he should buy a kilo of halva, five hundred grams of baklava, or a large and expensive French chocolate cake. But how on earth would he ever afford such things? He was nothing but a horse and he could never aspire to tasting or eating anything except for low-grade straw. The horse's face looked extremely sad now and his eyes drooped with a tragic sorrow.

Two trucks loaded with pistachio nuts (locally known as 'Aleppo nuts') became trapped behind him and started hooting their horns loud and furiously. Children appeared out of nowhere and started climbing all over the two trucks as well as the cart full of plums, then running off with bulging pockets and crunching teeth. Soon the red skins of fresh pistachios and the pips of plums began flying out from various windows onto the pavement, as mothers and grandmothers also began munching from behind the curtains. Then a freshly shaven young man came out of the sweet shop and held up a piece of candy floss in front of the horse's mouth, hoping to tempt him forward, but the horse stubbornly refused.

Then the most unexpected thing happened. As Dunya tried to take one last close-up photograph of the horse, another young man's face appeared in her lens. It was Hilal. By the time she had collected herself enough to believe the evidence of her eyes, the same young man had disappeared round a corner.

"Hilal! Hilal! Hilal!" Dunya called out his name, but her voice disappeared into the deafening din of the city. "Hilal!" She called out again and again and again, but he did not hear her and so she began to run behind him. Hilal took two rights, followed by three lefts and another right. He walked left, right, right, and then left. Finally he stopped in the middle of a group of men gathered outside an old-fashioned café.

Grand Café Taba
(Strictly Reserved for Men)

Now that she stood behind him, Dunya noticed that Hilal was wearing a fez. And when she moved around in order to look at his face—she saw his mustache. Despite this rather drastic change of appearance, Dunya recognized Hilal, but he seemed not to have recognized her.

What was the matter with him?

He was dressed in an old man's stripy suit and a pair of leather shoes she'd never seen him wear before. And he was shorter and slighter than most of the men around him. On closer inspection, Dunya noticed that he was no taller than her. How could this be Hilal? Yes, this young man certainly possessed Hilal's exact same eyes, his same black curly hair, and his general air . . . but he wasn't Hilal.

Dunya tried to stop herself from staring at this most confusing of young men, but it was too late, because he seemed to have finally noticed that she was looking at him, and was visibly delighted. She saw how he puffed up his chest with pride and ran his fingers through his hair with a vanity she had rarely seen in a man. She tried not to laugh. It was not Hilal. When she saw his cheeky face and how he winked at her and indicated to her with one of his fingers to come on over (presuming that she would do as she was told), she poked out her tongue at him. *What an arrogant young man. Who does he think he is?* Dunya thought to herself. *He needs to be taught a lesson.*

The young man burst out laughing. He was both startled and highly amused. Dunya was sure that no girl in Aleppo had ever poked her tongue out at him, let alone after pursuing him from street to street as she had done earlier. Everyone knew that it was the exclusive right and duty of a young man to look at and to pursue a girl, if it so pleased him, or to tease and taunt her if the mood took him; the other way round was a travesty.

The young man took his fez off and bowed down to Dunya, his curls almost touching the floor.

The men who stood outside Café Taba were now surrounding Hilal's lookalike and making a big fuss of him. Perhaps he was a well-known local figure or a public celebrity. An older man who looked like a dignitary kissed him on both cheeks and shook his hand, and the other men formed a corridor for him and whistled and smiled at him as he walked into the café to the sound of their loud and excited greetings.

And as for what happened next: if you happen to be the rational and scientific sort you might say, "Oh no, it cannot be. It cannot be! It could not have happened like this!"

But it can and it did.

Dunya decided that it could not be a simple coincidence that this young man looked so like Hilal. She'd been walking in Aleppo for hours and hours, and none of the men she'd seen in the city had looked anything like him. She must find out who he was. Was he related to Hilal? Perhaps he knew Hilal.

But by now the arrogant young man had stepped inside Café Taba and when Dunya tried to follow in his footsteps, the porter at the door blocked her entrance with his arms: "This is a men's-only café! Didn't you read the sign?" He shook his index finger authoritatively.

Dunya looked behind the porter's wall-like shoulders into Café Taba, which was bursting at the seams, almost exploding with men of all shapes and sizes, all clamoring to get a seat. Some were even sitting on one another's laps.

"What's happening? And who is this young man who just walked in?" Dunya asked him.

"He's Nijm the Hakawati, the youngest and best hakawati in the entire city of Aleppo. He's a singer and a philosopher too!" the porter announced pompously. (Of course the old towns of Aleppo and Damascus had always been famous for their troop of tireless hakawatis, the traditional storytellers who plied their trade in men's cafés).

"His name is Nijm? And he's a storyteller? And a singer too?" Dunya asked.

"Yes, one day he will be an international star, with a voice like his, and people will say that it was us here at Café Taba who first discovered him," the porter boasted.

"Can't you make an exception and let me in just for today? I'd like to hear his voice."

"Rules are rules young miss! When he's famous you'll be able to hear his songs on the radio, or you could buy one of his cassettes perhaps, but for now, he's exclusively *ours*," the porter said curtly.

"Is that so?" Dunya replied, before she walked confidently into Café Taba and disappeared into the crowd.

"What a cheek!" the porter mumbled to himself. "The girls of today are not like the girls of yesterday." But he busied himself welcoming more VIPs and guests and soon forgot all about Dunya.

Dunya hid behind a large column in the back of Café Taba and looked around trying to find Nijm.

"Nijm," she whispered his name to herself. *I wonder who he is? And why on earth he looks like a carbon copy of Hilal? I must find out, I need to know.*

Dunya watched as Café Taba was being transformed into a makeshift theater. All the chairs in the café were made to face a large table, on which there stood a chair.

A waiter put his finger on his lips, faced the audience, and said, "Shhhhh!"

Silence filled the café and the waiter opened a side door and from there appeared the handsome hakawati who climbed a stepladder next to the side of the table. He installed himself on the chair as if it were his throne and surveyed his audience from above.

Dunya looked at his curly black hair carefully, and she inspected his florid mustache and antique woollen fez, she observed his eyes and how he moved his fingers and his hands. Even from such close inspection she could still see what had first confused her so much about him—his uncanny resemblance to Hilal.

The hakawati rearranged his fez, as if it were some sort of crown, and from beneath his long and curly eyelashes he looked at the audience for a little while and then into the middle distance, as if he were about to say something.

But he didn't say a word.

Everyone watched him with entranced eyes, sucking and blowing on their hookahs—until he finally broke his silence with a cough.

"Good evening, my noble and chivalrous men. I hope you have braced yourselves today, for my tale will bring tears to your eyes and make you blush."

The audience clapped, puffing hookah smoke like chimneys.

The hakawati's voice was nothing like Hilal's voice.

"Gentlemen!" he said. "When will one of you offer his seat to our young lady guest? Why is she standing while you're all comfortably sitting on your asses?"

"A lady guest?" the men focused their gaze on Dunya and seemed taken aback for a moment or two. But then without exception they all stood up and gallantly offered her their seats.

"Come and sit here in front of me!" the hakawati said to Dunya. "So I can keep an eye on you. I like to see girls and women in this café, we need more of you. I congratulate you on your courage, Miss. It is a quality that is rare, in both men and women. Not even I have enough courage, if the truth be told," the Hakawati said. "Who might you be, Miss, and what brought you to our café? Is it simply wilfulness and a desire to shock, or do you have some other purpose? Come and sit on this chair, here in front of me!"

"I'm a photographer and my name is Dunya Noor," Dunya answered, choosing a chair that was positioned in front of the hakawati. Then she took her camera out of her bag.

"A photographer? I see. I've heard of their existence but I've never met one," the hakawati said. "Neither have I ever had my photograph professionally taken. May I order some copies from you?"

"Certainly," Dunya said.

Who are you? Dunya wished she could ask the hakawati right there and then. *I thought there was only one man in the world who looked like this, not two. . . .* Not only did the hakawati look like Hilal, but he also looked at her in the exact same way Hilal did—from beneath his long and curly eyelashes, as if he could see into her very soul.

"Do you," the hakawati asked the audience, "want me to tell you the Truth about Love?" he added while a waiter handed him an Arabic oud to play.

"Yes! For sure! Indeed! Yes! Of course! Indeed! For sure!" the audience cried out in a combination of baritone, monotone, tenor, countertenor, and bass voices—all expressing deep delight.

"Before I do that, you must first tell me something: do you all know and do you confess," the hakawati asked holding the oud next to his heart, "that there is not much difference between the human heart and an oud?"

"Yes, yes! We do know and we do confess!" the audience agreed in unison.

"They are similar both in shape and function," the hakawati said. "Both were made to sing." He touched his oud lovingly and then added, "I will sing my findings to you in three parts. Please serve me a glass of fresh tea between each part. Yes?"

"Your wish is our command," shouted a waiter.

"I will pretend to myself that the tea is a whisky," the hakawati said, smiling. "Spirits raise the spirit. But I am not advocating apostasy, remember that."

After that, the hakawati gently pulled on the first string of his oud and began to sing in a heavenly voice.

What is the Truth about Love
I scratched my chin, I drank some tea,
I looked in the sky and I looked in the sea.
I looked in a tin and I looked in the bin.
I looked in my pocket and I looked in my jacket.
I asked the rain and I wracked my brain.
I searched in vain!

I looked for it in silences and looked for it in words.
I shouted to the clouds and I asked passing birds.
I knew it must be hiding from me . . . because,
I couldn't find the Truth about Love.

So I asked my mother and I spoke to my father,
I questioned the young and talked to the old,
To hairy men and to those who were bald.
They told me that love was bad, very, very bad,
And that it had made them sad.

When Dunya heard the hakawati's voice, she almost fell off her chair: what sort of voice *was* this? When she looked behind her and around her, to her left and to her right, she saw that she was not the only one who felt it. The hakawati's song appeared to be making the audience slightly delirious; they were swaying gently left and right, as if trying not to dance. Their eyes were drawn heavenward, as if in a trance, and it was as if their hearts and their souls had sprung back to life (after a long sleep) with a force which left none of them in any doubt that they each possessed both a heart and a soul (a fact that prolonged periods of sadness, cynicism, and the chronic humdrumness of their daily lives had made them neglect and forget).

And then a bird that lives near my house decided to speak
and to open its mouth,
"Love is kept in a jam jar," it said,
"Somewhere under the staircase,
In a house by the hill where an old lady lives.
Love is invisible but it is like fire.
Run away from it, my son,
Run unless you want to be burnt!
Run away from love, my son,
Run unless you want to be hurt!
This is the Truth about Love," it said.

Every time the hakawati plucked at his oud, Dunya felt,
as everyone else in the café must have also felt, that he was
plucking directly at the strings of her heart.

Everyone inside Café Taba was mesmerized. Listening
to the hakawati's voice had the equivalent effect on each one
of them of drinking five shots of high-potency arak—in a
row. Even the waiter was so giddy and intoxicated with the
song that he held his copper tea-kettle at such a dangerous
angle, he almost started pouring its contents over a customer's head.

Dunya looked above her at the chandelier that hung from
the old café's ceilings and wished that she had not lost her way
in Aleppo. It would soon be dark outside, and what would she
do if she did not find Hilal tonight, and if the hakawati had
never heard of him?

But then, on the other hand, being here, listening to the
hakawati sing about love and asking questions she'd always
asked herself, using the exact same words, gave her a sense
that this could not be an accident, that walking into this café
was part of her quest, not only to find Hilal.

Dunya couldn't wait to hear what the hakawati's findings
were.

"Why should I believe this strange bird's words?" The hakawati's voice filled Café Taba and all the hearts of its customers. "Why should I, my love?"

"Why? Why?" the audience asked.

Fear is the opposite of Love,
As Lies are the opposite of Truth!
It is "You," my darling, who is the Truth about Love.
It is "You" who holds the key.
The word "Yes," my darling, is the Truth about Love.
And "No" is the secret of Pain.
Say, "Yes," my darling,
Be mine again.

The customers of Café Taba were tapping their feet on the floor, up and down, following the beats of the hakawati's song.

The hakawati gulped his third glass of tea, and then continued to sing in his alluring voice, which gave his audience goose pimples, making even the stoniest-hearted of them almost want to cry.

No one knew why.

None of the audience could take their eyes off him, nor could they stop listening to every word and every syllable he uttered even though they were sure that he knew nothing about Love. He was clearly too young and too vain and had never suffered. Even Dunya was sure of it. None of them could fully or even partially understand the theories he was trying to peddle through the vehicle of his songs. How could Fear be the opposite of Love? Wasn't Hate its eternal enemy and opposite? The hakawati was talking nonsense, trying to be clever, they were sure of that. Even Dunya who thought of herself (relatively speaking) as an expert on the theories of Love and its manifold manifestations did not understand. But none of them really cared whether he was right or wrong because what they loved about him most of all were not his stories, or his theories, nor his rhymes—but the *voice* in which he sang them. Perhaps in Europe or America people could follow their hearts, some of the men reasoned. But here, in the conservative Republic of Syria, Fear was the master. Fear held everything and everyone under its sway, and everyone respectfully bowed their heads to it.

The audience clapped and clapped and clapped, while a tall, slim, manic-depressive looking waiter replenished their hookahs. Then someone said, "These are not stories for men. Tell us one about the warriors of Arabia!"

"I'll tell you one about the genie who lost his bottle! That's a story you'll love. But I think it must wait until tomorrow. On Friday I'll read to you from the ancient story of Antar and Abla." The hakawati winked.

"Another love story?" shouted the waiter.

Everyone looked flushed. His subject matter, which was often and forever Love, was of no interest to them but, despite their frequent protests, they always came back for more. Even the clients of another competing hakawati café were emigrating to Café Taba in hordes. It was shameful and unfair. The hakawati was drawing them in like flies. Was it his unusually entrancing voice? Was it his piercing and passionate eyes? No one knew. He was just a random young man who happened to be a master of spectacle and song and who skilfully, but cruelly, knew how to hold them under his spell.

Suddenly a middle-aged man with a particularly long handlebar mustache stood up: "I don't understand why, for goodness sake, I mean, why? Why are you singing to us about birds that speak?" He stood up, exposing a very large and round belly that had clearly been nurtured on a lethal and regular diet of stuffed eggplant. "I mean, Sir, are we children that you sing to us of such things?" He reached for his hookah and took a puff. "Nor are we women, for that matter, that we want to hear of Love."

"Do men not think of Love then?" the hakawati said in a surprised and chastising tone. "I don't believe it." He stood up on the table and swayed a little, as if to find his balance. "Is it men who write most love songs and love poetry or is it women? You tell me!" he demanded. "You do have a lot to learn, before you truly understand what a man is. A man who doesn't love is no such thing, and a man is not as different from a woman as you might like to convince yourselves."

The audience made no suggestion of sound.

"So you're not a hakawati then," the mustachioed man said. "You're a teacher."

"I'm not a teacher, make no such mistake," the hakawati said confidently. "I'm a Professor—a Professor of Love."

What a peacock and a dandy! Dunya adored everything about Nijm. He seemed nothing like other young men in the city, not even like Hilal who wasn't theatrical like that and not so verbose and spectacular.

"Are you lot good at mathematics?" the hakawati asked the audience.

"Of course we are," the audience composed mainly of shopkeepers and such insisted.

"The world is mathematics, some things are systematic. A mathematical turn of mind, the ability to be calculating and to make correct calculations, is very beneficial when one is in the throes of trying to survive the trials and tribulations of an impossible love," the hakawati declared. "Here is my lesson for all you people with heartache. Have any of you, by the way, ever suffered heartache?" the hakawati asked.

"No way!" the audience cried.

"That is what they all say!" The hakawati looked at his audience and continued:

"A Lesson in Emotional Mathematics—or the Mathematics of Love.

"$L + O + V + E = ?$

"I collected the letters 'l,' 'o, ' 'v, ' and 'e' and looked at them all separately. They were only four. They were so easy to write, so easy to pronounce, so easy to look at or glance at. But why could the state they describe not be easy, too? Two? The answer might be three."

The hakawati made the shape of a triangle with his hands.

"One + One = Love.

"One + One + One = Pain.

"In love, One + Two = Zero

"Love is a game, which only pairs can play."

The café burst into a frenzy of claps.

"We have been told that to be happy each one of us must only love *one* thing, must always give our heart entirely to the *One* we love, and that a heart can never be divided by two or three or four *or more*," the Hakawati lectured. "We have been ordered and repeatedly told that we must only worship one god, blindly follow one leader, that we should only be loyal to one nation, only obey one father and honor one mother—everyone else we must hate. Why can't we love both black and white, worship both day and night. Why do we have to choose only *one*? One is a lonely number."

Nijm now plucked at his oud strings tragically as the audience looked at him. They began to huff and puff rather nervously.

What was the hakawati trying to say? they wondered. Did he not believe in one god any more, did he not agree that Hafez al-Assad was Syria's only possible leader or was he trying in a rather convoluted but polite way to advocate polygamy? Everyone hoped and prayed that it was the latter, because only the latter was acceptable and permissible—in the ancient souk of Aleppo, everything else was blasphemy or treason. The men of Café Taba loved the hakawati so much that they did not want to think of what might happen to him were he to be accused of some ineffable thought-crimes against religion or the state.

"Come drink another cup of tea," the waiter said to him. "And stop giving us all a headache!"

The hakawati's eyebrows were highlighted in a dramatic way and the lapels of his shirt flew out to the sides in an endearingly pretentious manner. He had both humor and glamor, something rarely seen in typical staid hakawatis who were always and forever in the autumn of their lives.

"How do you do it?" one of the men asked the hakawati. "How do you manage to hypnotize us with your lies, young sir?"

"These are not lies, I promise you, boys. I only sing about the truth. All I have in my profession are the twenty-eight letters of the Arabic alphabet. With them I must capture your hearts and souls. I think of them the same way a musician thinks of his musical notes. These are not lies, I promise you, boys. I only sing about the truth, your heart's truth."

"We're not boys," the audience protested all together in unison, like boys in a classroom.

Dunya looked at the strange assortment of men sitting on rickety chairs all around her, some holding their bellies as if in anticipation of what the hakawati might say next, while others tried to rearrange their hairdos in an attempt to look as alluring as possible, possibly as alluring as the hakawati himself. He seemed to be reminding them of how they could or might have been. He effortlessly outshone them all and that was not something they were used to from a hakawati. For normally a hakawati was a dusty and rather rusty man, not so young and full of himself. And if he happens to be young, he should not be so jumped up and pleased with himself, but must be respectful of those who are older than him, and in awe of them! This young man broke all the rules.

The hakawati watched Dunya take photographs of everyone in the café as if she didn't think it was an issue. Most of the men thought that she should have at least asked them if they minded but they were too shy or polite to say anything.

With her green eyes and light brown hair and unusually scruffy dress-sense, Dunya appeared European, and so they saw her as a woman who operated outside their realm of rules and regulations. They were feeling very spaced-out and open-minded in any case that evening and everything seemed acceptable and possible to them.

Dunya focused her lens on the hakawati's face. He was smiling directly at her. He had long and curving eyelashes that he fluttered at her mockingly. "Look at this girl!" he pointed his finger at Dunya. "She's taking photos of all and sundry without asking for permission. Shouldn't we have a say in whether she's allowed to steal our images from the air like this or not? But no, we're gentlemen after all and we'll submit to her curiosity, won't we? We're not afraid of a girl who might or might not be a thief of light, who might or might not be taking pieces of our souls, our hearts, and dreams, and storing them inside that machine she's holding. We're men and so we don't worry about subtle, ephemeral things like this, do we?" The hakawati waved his book in the air. "Did you not know that the soul is made of light? And photography, I'll have you know, is the art of capturing light inside a machine, capturing it and making it everlasting."

"What fresh crop of new nonsense is this? I don't believe a word of it," a man with a white mustache and stripy clothes said.

"Well, what's your answer, girl?" the hakawati asked Dunya. "Are you nothing but a thief of light? The boys here would like to know."

"Light," Dunya said looking around her at the strange assortment of mustaches waiting in anticipation for her answer. "Light is something subtle but infinite. If I take some I'm not stealing because it comes from a fountain whose supply is like a never-ending tap of water. I only take a drop and I only do it so that something beautiful can be seen later by others. Do you really think this is stealing?" Dunya addressed the men.

The audience clapped and clapped and clapped, while a barrel-shaped, angry-looking waiter replenished their hookahs. Finally, he brought Dunya her own hookah as a mark of respect and solidarity. "This is a honey-scented one for you, my dear."

When the show was over the hakawati jumped off the table and walked toward Dunya.

"And what brings you here, young lady?" he asked her playfully. "Is it me? Did someone send you to take a picture of me and if so, who was it?"

"Well," Dunya said. "I came to Aleppo looking for a man who looks almost exactly like you, but he is not you. The young astronomy student Hilal Shihab. At first I thought you were him. Might you have heard of him?"

Now that he stood so close to her Dunya noticed how Nijm's features were more delicate than Hilal's, and how his hands were so much smaller. She tried to compose herself. This was easily one of the strangest incidents she had experienced in her still rather young life. She had never before heard of anyone have such a thing happen to them.

Nijm looked at Dunya as if she had asked him the strangest of questions.

"Isn't Hilal Shihab the only son of Said and Suad, the tailor and seamstress, and does he not live abroad?" he said in a trembling voice.

"Yes that's *him*!"

Dunya was about to jump up and down from joy and had to stop herself from putting her arms around Nijm in celebration of that good news.

"You say that I look like him, so much so that you mistook me for him?" Nijm scratched his ear in disbelief.

"Yes," Dunya said. "The only difference is that you're a little shorter than him and you dress very differently. And he does not have a mustache . . . but, as for the rest, you could be brothers."

"This is the oddest thing I have heard for a very long time," Nijm smiled. "So very, very odd and strange."

"Do you know where his parents live?"

"Yes," Nijm said. "They live on Plum Street. Would you like me to take you there?"

"Please," Dunya said.

Nijm looked contemplative for a moment as if he was trying to make up his mind about something. "As it happens I've been meaning to visit Hilal's parents for a while now, but then I heard about his father's passing away and didn't want to intrude on his mother. But I have a question to ask her."

"What sort of question?" Dunya asked.

"The first *I* heard of Mr. and Mrs. Shihab and their son was when I received a delivery of an exceptionally well-made outfit, a product of their skilled hands . . . more than six months ago now. And as I never went for a fitting, how could it be explained that the outfit fit me so perfectly, every line and every curve? Additionally, I never ordered the outfit, nor paid for it. Wouldn't you say that this is most improbable and strange? And then to add to the conundrum, you appear in my life like a vision in a dream and your first words to me are related to their son. And you say that I am the spitting image of him. There must be an answer to all of this, wouldn't you agree? I'd like to ask Mrs. Shihab about it," Nijm said matter-of-factly.

That afternoon Dunya walked out of Café Taba in the company of the young and handsome hakawati in front of a throng of disapproving men, of all shapes and sizes, all ages, all religious and political persuasions—but they all agreed on one thing: "Foreign women!" they muttered to one another.

"Even this one who looks so innocent, look at her, she just goes off with any stranger! If my daughter did that I'd flatten her," one of them said after a moment of silence.

"That hakawati is cheeky. *I* wanted to ask her to come with me. Presumptuous fool! Who does he think he is?" said another.

"He's a sly young thing. All these love stories. I bet you he tries to practice what he preaches on unsuspecting young women. Keep your wives locked up, guys. Keep the key somewhere secret."

16

A Girl Like No Other

THIS CITY WAS FAR TOO strange, and far too mysterious, much stranger and more mysterious than any other city Dunya had ever set foot in. She felt as if a deep and eternal song filled it, a song that had begun before the world was born, a song that never stopped being sung and had never been interrupted. It was a silent song, but everywhere she went she imagined she could hear it. Its beat was that of a heartbeat, its melody that of a sigh, and its shape that of a beautiful young woman who loved to dance both day and night, regardless of whether it was dark or light, and who did not care a fig whether anyone was watching.

One alley came after the other, each one following the other from unexpected corners. Beautiful noises, throngs of people, crowds, smells of pepper, flour, dust, oranges, and donkeys' feet. How beautiful chaos could be, how freeing to have so many uneven lines, to walk on a ground that wasn't insulated from the earth by hundreds of layers, to feel the heart of a city beating.

"Here we are!" Nijm announced as he stood in front of an old bakery, sandwiched between a series of dilapidated and dusty-looking apartments.

The Aleppo Central Bakery
Est. 1945 By Habibi & Sons

"But Hilal doesn't live next to a bakery," Dunya said.

"Yes, I know, but I do," Nijm said. "Before I take you to Hilal's house, I'd like to change into the outfit which his parents made me. And I'd like you to meet my wife, love of my life. Wouldn't you like to meet her?" the hakawati pointed to a door underneath the bakery at the bottom of some steps.

"You have a wife?" Dunya found this hard to believe. Nijm looked so young and so irresponsible. "Can't I meet her another day? I'm in a hurry to find Hilal, I've been looking for him since this morning."

"Hilal's house is only a stone's throw away. Just come in for a minute, and then we'll be on our way, I promise." Nijm smiled. "You're a pretty girl and if Khadija hears of me walking up and down the city streets with you, I'll never hear the end of it." Nijm laughed. "I'll make you a glass of my special lemonade while you wait for me, or a cup of tea. I'm famous for my special lemonade and for my mind-blowing tea." Nijm rolled the tip of his mustache around one of his fingers, as if this was an invitation that would be impossible to resist.

"Maybe another time," Dunya said.

Nijm stared at Dunya and she stared back at him, and for a moment their eyes met and she felt that she was at risk of falling into them. He had beautiful deep black eyes. And he fluttered them at her. Why did he flutter them like that? And why was he looking at her like this, in that exact same way Hilal looked at her, with those exact same eyes? There was no way in the world now that she would go into his apartment with him. *There is only one Hilal in this world, and this man is not him. I don't want, nor do I need, two Hilals. One is all I need.* She quickly averted her eyes from him.

"If you come in I promise you I won't touch you, not even with a feather. I promise. Please say yes. Say yes."

"No," Dunya said. "And in any case what sort of young man invites a young woman he just met to come into his apartment? And what sort of young woman would say yes?"

"Normally it is not done, I know, I know. I'm a traditional young man and I accept our customs. The reason I wish you'd come into my house with me is because, well, I'm very good at making tea and I think you'd love my tea, but if you try my special lemonade, then you will be hooked on it. As I mentioned earlier, I make the best lemonade in Aleppo. Is that not a good reason? And I want you to meet my wife, as I said, and I want her to meet you. I really, really do," Nijm smiled cheekily. "I swear upon my mother Basma and her soft and gentle heart, and upon the honor of Khadija and her long black tresses, that I am an honorable young man. I'm not an immoral and heartless hunter of girls, if that is what you think."

"I don't believe you," Dunya said in a determined voice.

"I swear that I'm not."

"You look as if you are. Can't you just write Hilal's address on a piece of paper and then I can go and find him myself?"

"I could," Nijm said. "Yes, I could, but I'd like to go with you. I want to meet Hilal and his mother, and I want you to introduce me to them." Nijm took a deep breath and in what looked like a final desperate attempt he said the following: "In any case, even if I didn't have a wife and if I was looking for a girl to seduce, you'd not be my type, I swear it. I see you more as a sister. And be sure that if any harm came to you, the entire congregation of Café Taba would point their fingers at me and I'd become a social and artistic pariah. That's not my life's ambition. I want to be a singer and a star, and I think you might be able to help me. Consider me your brother. I don't have a sister."

"You're a strange boy," Dunya said. "And so insistent and pushy. I don't usually like pushy people, and neither does Hilal. He might really hate you, you know."

"I'm sure he'll like me," Nijm rolled the tip of his mustache dreamily. "Everyone does."

"Do they?" Dunya couldn't believe her ears. This young man really had a rather inflated ego, but he was making her laugh. She'd never met such an annoying and smug young man and in the end her curiosity got the better of her. So after insisting that she take his set of keys from him as her guarantee, they went down the steps into his underground apartment.

Both Nijm and Dunya now stood in the middle of a large room full of bags of flour stacked to a great height. There was a collection of cushions, which were arranged like a sofa in the middle. On the right wall there were shelves full of books of every shape and size, and on the left wall there was a large cupboard filled to bursting with clothes. On a third wall there was a long mirror and next to it a small mirror and next to that a tap above a white basin. Dunya turned around slowly in order to survey the room. She kept turning and turning and turning. "Why do you have so many bags of flour everywhere? And where is your darling wife, the love of your life?"

Nijm followed her quietly and then stood face to face with her. "If you stop turning around," he said bossily, "I'll tell you." He looked at her in a sly way, half-closing his eyes. He seemed to be examining her through his soft and rather long eyelashes, up and down as if trying to make up his mind about her. He then clasped his mustache, paused a little, dropped his hands, and, "Hmm," he hummed.

"Hmm, what?" Dunya asked him.

"They say that girls with overly curly hair have a tendency to be reckless," he said in a thoughtful tone. "And I must say in your case at least it is true, so true!" Nijm laughed.

"I am curious, not reckless."

"No?" Nijm didn't seem convinced. "Whatever pleases you to think, think it, but the truth is that you are reckless. And not only that, but also feckless."

"Feckless?" Dunya said. "You on the other hand are smug and vain, most vain and smug, and will I also soon be finding out that you are a liar?"

"A liar?" Nijm said. "No, not a liar."

"So if you are not a liar, where is your wife then, love of your life?"

"She's on her way. Khadija! Khadija! Come down, Khadija!" Nijm called out.

The hakawati called his wife, once, twice, and one more time but she didn't appear to hear him.

"There is no Khadija, is there?" Dunya said. "Didn't I tell you you're a liar?"

"Look, Dunya," Nijm said in a serious tone. "I am grateful that you trusted me enough to come into my apartment with me. I don't know what it is about you, but as I said before I was so taken and impressed by how you came into Café Taba and your boldness and courage that there and then I decided we must be friends. But friendship without truthfulness is not possible and therefore I also in that same instant decided I would tell you the truth about myself. But before telling it, I had to make up a little lie. I hope you'll forgive me."

"What truth?" Dunya asked Nijm. "What lie?"

"Well, . . ." Nijm said.

"Well what?"

"Well, well, well. What the hell." Nijm took the middle of his mustache between two of his fingers and then without any warning he ripped it off his face—*whoosh!*

Nijm's ornate mustache came off his upper lip very easily and didn't leave a trace. He held it up in the air, and swung it above his head proudly as if it were a mouse he'd just caught.

Then he put it in his trouser pocket.

"Your mustache is not real?" Dunya was startled. "You're in disguise?"

"Yes, Dunya. I'm not who I appear to be, nor what you think you can see," he said in a soft and melodious voice.

"Your voice," Dunya said.

"What about it?" Nijm asked playfully.

"You have a girl's voice." Dunya fixed her eyes on him.

"Certainly not a boy's," Nijm repeated in that exquisitely feminine and sensuous voice, which was completely different from the one he'd used before. "I told you you had nothing to worry about, didn't I?" He took his fez off and flung it away, along with something Dunya had imagined—only seconds ago—to be his hair.

Long luscious black locks were set free.

Nijm then ran to the tap in the corner and washed his face, splashing water here and there. He then sat down on a chair and dried his cheeks and forehead with a freshly laundered white towel.

"What's your name?" Dunya asked.

"Suha," she said.

What had at first appeared to Dunya to be a handsome young man was nothing of the sort, because the truth of it was that she was a ravishingly beautiful young woman.

Why did she hide herself, Dunya wondered? *There must be a reason for her intricate disguise. Did she do it to protect herself from others, or to protect others from herself? She was everything that inspired love; how could anyone resist her? How could anyone not want her for themselves, want to fall at her feet and love her?* Dunya imagined how a girl like Suha walking down the street or singing in the cafés of Aleppo might cause a riot, numberless street battles and fist fights would ensue, as well as shootings and intense and protracted gang warfare. She was that beautiful.

And as for her voice, her real voice with which she spoke as her real self—it was utterly beguiling and expressed a perfect picture of her soul, adding to the fatal mixture of her beauty and impossible charm, a lethal ingredient.

There was a velvety silence that filled the room now. Suha took her men's shoes off and put them near the door. Her bone structure, her stature, and her height were all those of a girl. She was not a boy, not a young man. He was not a he, but a perfectly exquisite *she*. Dunya could not quite get to grips with this sudden change in Nijm's identity and appearance. It was like a hallucination. She looked at Suha as she took her tie off and unbuttoned her jacket. She moved so differently and behaved so distinctly from how she did before; everything about her was different from Nijm, except a certain irresistible attractiveness, which was the same. What a good actress she was! Dunya felt confused and yet privileged that Suha had decided so whimsically and for no apparent reason to reveal her true self to her. What did she want from her?

Dunya sat down on a cushion and took a deep breath. "I want to hear your story. Tell me everything," she said.

Suha came nearer to her and sat on a cushion opposite her. "Are you sure you want to hear it now? Or shall I just wear the dress Suad sent me and then we can go and find Hilal?"

"Was it a dress that she sent you?"

"Yes," Suha said.

"So Hilal's parents know you as a girl?"

"It seems they do," Suha said.

"Do you think they wanted to introduce him to you or you to him, because they're hoping you might become his wife one day?" Dunya asked fearfully.

"No, I'm sure it's not that, it's something entirely different. Don't worry, I won't try to snatch Hilal away from you," Suha said. "He is your sweetheart, isn't he?"

But Dunya was not sure how anyone, even Hilal, would not fall in love with Suha at first sight. And her heart sank.

Clearly if she was going to bring Suha to Hilal's house, she would need much courage. It would be the ultimate test of his love. If he truly loved her, Suha would not touch him in any way. If he truly loved her, not even a girl as stunning as Suha would be able to steal his love away from her. Dunya looked at Suha and felt rather faint.

She could see that Suha was a heartbreaker. Only a very brave man would dare to love her. To love her would require enormous amounts of courage and perhaps a sprinkle, or a good dose, of madness. What a risk loving her would be, what a knife's edge.

"What I don't understand," Suha said, "is how could I have invented an imaginary young man who looks so like your Hilal, a man I never met?" Suha took a brush from a dresser nearby and began to brush her hair.

"I wonder too," Dunya said, hoping that this was not some sort of uncanny coincidence whereby Suha created the man of her own dreams. "Tell me, then," she asked her, "do you have a sweetheart or a fiancée?"

"Sometimes I do," Suha said. "But at the moment I don't. I've looked and looked for true love, but I haven't found it yet. Is Hilal your One True Love or just a passing infatuation?"

"He is my One True Love," Dunya said.

"I've never been in love like that with anyone. My heart has always been a difficult instrument, impossible to master. You must teach me what you know about love."

"Me teach you?" Dunya blushed. "I don't think I'll have anything to teach you."

"I know it requires courage, and I don't have enough of that," Suha said. "That's my problem. I'm too cowardly, true love requires enormous courage, they say."

"I suppose it does," Dunya said. "Or enormous recklessness." She smiled at Suha. "So how did you learn how to disguise yourself so well as a young man, when you're a beautiful woman?" Dunya watched Suha as she continued to brush her hair.

"My mustache was made in Paris," Suha said as if by way of explanation, "by a mustache professional. And my fez was smuggled in from Turkey in 1922, the year when Mustafa Kemal Atatürk banned the fez in the newly born Republic. Did you know that since the fez was banned in Turkey, Turkish men were forced to hide their Oriental natures under European berets and bowler hats? I'm not the only one who must hide my true self. What is true is often illegal in this country, and also elsewhere in the world. One could easily get killed for it," Suha said. Her feminine voice reverberated through the room and touched everything in it.

"But why hide that you're a girl?" Dunya asked Suha, "It's not illegal to be a girl in this city, is it? Tell me who you are and why you live like this?"

"I'll tell you who I am, perhaps another day."

"No, tell me now."

"Now?" Suha took a bottle of perfume from a drawer and sprayed a little on her wrist. "I need to get rid of that boy smell," she said, "the smell of old men and cigarettes and hookahs and mustaches and teahouses before I can tell anyone anything. So you tell me, how did Hilal capture your heart?"

Dunya tried to think of how she might explain her love for Hilal to Suha, but she found that she could not concentrate on the subject and that she had no idea what to say about it or what she actually thought of it. All her feelings, all her thoughts, all her ideas, all memories, all images and theories of love had evaporated from her mind and she could not make head nor tail of any of them. All she was conscious of was sitting there in that room with this girl she had never met before and whose name was Suha. Was Suha not the name of a distant star that could not be seen with human eyes? She remembered that Hilal had once mentioned it to her.

Suha crossed one of her legs over the other, and then she yawned. "As it's so hot here, let me make you my special lemonade instead of a glass of tea." She picked up a couple of tall blue glasses from a cupboard and from a fridge pulled out a bottle of cold water.

Dunya watched Suha squeeze one lemon and then another and pour their contents between the two glasses. She pulled a spoon out of a small wooden drawer and found a bag of sugar. A silence filled the large room and the small space that separated them. Dunya listened to the sound of Suha's spoon touching the tall glasses. It was very hot, almost too hot as this room had probably not been aired for a long time, and there weren't any fans. Dunya looked at Suha's bare feet and the nail varnish on her toes and realized that she far preferred her as a girl. She wanted to be her friend, to talk to her, she wanted to know everything about her from the beginning to the end. They would need to have many conversations, conversations that might take years. She was sure of it. One afternoon could never be enough.

Suha breathed, slowly, so slowly, so leisurely, as if she were inhaling an invisible cigarette whose smoke filled her soul and made her dream, and when she breathed out, that same smoke surrounded Dunya and brought her against her will into Suha's strange and mysterious orbit. Oh, she liked her. She liked her. Everything about her.

Dunya sat down on the floor next to Suha and the two of them innocently stared at each other for a moment or two, or three or more. One, two, three, four—one, two, three, four. They stared at one another like this for a moment, or two, and then three, and then four. But neither of them knew what to say, or how to describe that moment, or understand it.

Suha rested her back on a cushion and began to tell Dunya why she had decided to disguise herself as a young man.

"I'm sure you must've discovered in your travels that it's men who rule the world? And that only a man has the right to speak, whereas a young woman is mostly expected to be silent." She picked up a sunflower seed from a bowl next to her and cracked it between her teeth. "Why is it that only they can speak, only they can think, only they can sing, only they can look, that we must be their objects? I've never understood or accepted the injustice of this, but I've always known it to be true," she said. "Dressed as a young man no one expects anything from me and I can do as I please. Everyone listens to me rather than being distracted by my bosom, my legs, my ass."

"What if someone discovers you're a girl? Aren't you afraid of being discovered?"

"Of course I'm afraid," Suha said. "Nothing worth doing is *not* terrifying. . . . But if it's worth doing then it must be done, otherwise life isn't worth living. When my father passed away last year my mother brought down all his old suits and put them in this basement here." Suha pointed to the ancient wooden wardrobe. "I don't know how it came about but I opened the wardrobe one day and began to look at his old clothes and I remembered when he used to take me out on visits and buy me chocolates and ice creams. He was a slim man and shorter than usual and I realized I could easily fit into his suits. I took my dress off and put on a suit of his. Then I tried on a pair of his good quality leather shoes and his favorite fez. I looked in the mirror and didn't recognize myself. I moved my feet roughly, my shoulders proudly, and my chin in a manly fashion. You know what I mean? If you observe them closely you'll notice they do everything a little differently from us, there's a lot more ego and self-importance in their movements. They often possess what one might call 'panache,' especially the men here in our neighborhood. I went shopping for a few items in a theater shop I'd seen next to the national theater. Soon enough I'd collected mustaches, eyebrows, neck hair, ear hair, an Adam's apple, a couple of artificial warts and about three makes of men's cologne, as well as ten different types of makeup, which I learned how to mix to create the right skin tone. I found that after putting on a hat I was able to slip out of the house looking like a young gentleman. I called myself Nijm. I thought of Nijm as the brother I always wished I had. Dressed like him, I found that Aleppo turned into something much tastier than I'd been used to. Aleppo had tasted like a plain biscuit to me before. But now it tasted like nothing less than an open box of delicious Turkish delight. It was instantly transformed from a strict and tyrannical chaperone, who watched over me with hawk-like eyes, to a rowdy and entertaining companion. It was no longer a city where I had to walk with eyes averted from everything around me, a city where I couldn't strike up conversations with passersby or sit in cafés drinking tea and listening to gossip or to professional storytellers. What a transformation a suit and a fez can make to the life of a young woman. When I discovered how much fun I could have just by pretending to be someone else and by treating the streets and local shops and cafés like a theater, I couldn't give up that delicious freedom. I decided from then on to recycle my father's old suits and hats into costumes for my own private play."

"But what about your voice?" Dunya asked her with incredulity. "How could you fake that?"

"At first I pretended I was mute or pathologically taciturn, then I learned to speak like a man. That took a while of practicing in front of the mirror with the help of an old tape recorder. I smoked endless cigarettes to add texture to my voice."

"I find this hard to believe," Dunya said.

"The taste of freedom made me fearless. When I walked around Aleppo dressed as a young man—casually smoking a cigarette—most people looked at me and asked, 'A new visitor? Will he be doing business with one of us? Is he into pistachios or jewelery?' When I'd passed by them as a girl their reactions were always very different, most of their comments about me had always been either of the lustful or else of the finger-pointing variety. As a girl, one has to be perfect at all times. A girl isn't allowed to be too attractive or too ugly. It's considered outrageous for a girl to be too stupid or too intelligent. Anything exceptional about a woman seems to be considered a sort of affront to men or to other women. And as for singing, forget it! A female singer is often regarded as the vocal equivalent of a prostitute or a stripper. A woman's voice is considered by the religiously *enlightened* to be as erotic as her naked body, and so they consider it her duty to hide it from them in order to protect them from its seductive power.

"As a man, nothing seemed to matter, all graces became multiplied and all disgraces an honor—a man with a beautiful voice is an asset to society and to his nation, and so I had no other choice. Finally I could breathe and laugh and walk with a long confident stride and look at the world squarely in the eye. As Nijm, I began to frequent Café Taba and to listen to its hakawatis and that's when I found my once-in-a-lifetime opportunity.

"My heart's desire has always been to be a singer or a performer of some kind but I've always been forbidden from pursuing it, though it's the only real desire I was born with and I don't know how to get rid of it. The only audience I could ever dream of having were three people: my mother and my two cousins, who are always adoring and always clap. Even though I know I might never become a real singer and perform in public, I still want to grow and improve my voice and my talent. I don't want them to wither and die. How could I ever believe I'm good if I don't test my talent against a real audience composed of uncaring and cold-hearted strangers? So I took my oud and went to see Hassoun the manager of Café Taba. I had to bribe him of course to begin with—with a box of halva and two bottles of expensive arak—otherwise Mr. Hassoun would not have listened to me or given me an audition. My first show was an instant success and after that the customers always asked for me. And so now Mr. Hassoun has to bribe *me* to keep me at his café and to make sure I don't stray to a competing establishment. He buys me packets of cigarettes or anything I ask of him. Cups of tea mainly."

As she spoke, Suha's voice reverberated through Dunya's mind and soul and imagination, and filled every part of her, like a beautiful song, impossible to resist. Dunya looked at Suha and instead of feeling fear or dread or panic or rivalry, or worrying whether Hilal might fall in love with her, she felt wonder, perfect wonder.

"What a beautiful story," she said. "Hard to believe. But I believe you."

"This is only a small part of it," Suha said. "There's so much more which I'd like to tell you one day. But I wonder why I'm telling you all this when I've never told it to anyone else before, and never thought I ever would, and I don't even know you.

"Do you always blush so much? Why are you blushing?"

"I'm not blushing. I don't blush."

"You are blushing." With the tip of her finger, Suha touched the tip of Dunya's burning cheek. "Or perhaps I need to open the window. It is too hot down here, isn't it?"

Yes it was hot, far too hot. The heat filled Dunya. She felt it in her throat, then in her heart, it spread through her lungs, circled inside her stomach, moved through her hair, touched her hands, and traveled all the way down to her feet. It burned her body.

Suha took a plastic bag from a box and from it she picked out a yellow dress and rested it on a chair beside her. "I'll put Mr. and Mrs Shihab's dress on, if you don't mind, and then we can ask Suad about it. What do you say?"

She slowly unbuttoned her father's white shirt and his black trousers. She was wearing nothing but her underwear now. Who would have imagined that underneath that young man's suit would be the body of possibly the most beautiful young woman in Aleppo? Her limbs were long and luscious, her arms, her breasts. Dunya felt ashamed of herself. Why was she looking at her like that? Was she admiring her or was she envying her, or fearing her, or wanting to be like her? She had no idea. Suha folded the shirt and hung it inside a cupboard and then did the same with the trousers. Dunya now only dared to look at Suha's body in parts, not all at once. Every part of her body—her shoulders, her legs, her stomach, her hips, her feet, her hands, her hair—was like a song, like a wave, like the wind, beautiful beyond measure.

The yellow dress fitted Suha perfectly and seemed to hold her like a lover's hand. It followed the contours of her body and seemed to bring out the qualities of her very *soul*.

Or that was how the yellow dress appeared in Dunya's eyes. She noticed how much more light the dress brought out of Suha, who was already so brilliant and so bright. The closer Suha came toward Dunya the more brightly she glittered. And as Dunya continued to look at her, she saw how Suha's bright light appeared to fill the enormous high-ceilinged room from top to bottom. She looked like a star that had come down to the city of Aleppo on that hot summer evening for a short visit.

Suha turned her back to Dunya, "Will you help me zip it up?" she said. With the edges of her fingers Dunya zipped up Suha's dress, trying not to touch her.

How could she be so sure that what she saw in Suha that afternoon was not simply a trick of the light?

Suha was looking at Dunya as Dunya looked at her. No woman had ever looked at her like that. Why was Suha looking at her like this, like *that*, in that way? Perhaps she looked at everything like this: at a box of matches, at a spoon, at a bird perched above her window, at the moon. Suha seemed to be looking at Dunya as if she thought she could have her heart if she wanted to. And what an unsettling look it was! One moment passed followed by the next one and the next one. Dunya could not believe what her eyes could see, nor what her heart was feeling.

"If you were a boy, I swear I'd kiss you," Suha said. "You're far too pretty as a girl ever to be a boy, but I hope one day I'll meet a boy like you."

What a thing to say. Dunya couldn't believe that Suha had said that, and she was too startled to reply.

"I like your soft green eyes. I'll look for a young man with eyes like that. If you find one, tell him to come and find me," Suha said.

Dunya tried to hold herself upright, to pretend that everything was alright. She tried to smile lightly as if she did not have a care in the world, she tried not to cry, even though she could feel her tears coming. Now she knew that Suha would only bring her sorrow.

"I hope you stay long enough in Aleppo for us to become friends," Suha said.

"I hope so too."

"Let's go and find Hilal."

And this was how in one summer's afternoon black turned to white, dark turned to light, a boy turned into a girl, and the love which Dunya had once given to Hilal was no longer his.

Hilal now seemed pale like the moon in Dunya's eyes, while Suha was bright and blinding like the sun when it comes too near.

No one had ever told her such a thing could happen, no one had said.

Beautiful girl, you're the one I love, Dunya thought to herself as she looked at Suha.

17

What the Coffee Cup Said

Mrs. Suad Shihab came back home that morning carrying a heavy plastic bag full of the best-quality Egyptian linen cloth she could find. *Today my son will come,* she kept repeating to herself. She was about to make Hilal a suit that could hold him as if in her hands and protect him from everything bad in this world—a white suit that might shield him from the dark. She'd bought this length of superior-quality white linen at the wholesalers in the north of Aleppo and she'd selected six white, matte buttons. She'd bought thread the color of shadows and a special new pencil to draw the lines of her designs with. As soon as she closed the door behind her, Suad went to her cutting table and laid out the length of white cloth in the proper position. With her new pencil she drew dark lines: his shoulders, his neck, his chest. She took her black scissors from a drawer underneath—and began cutting.

Said. Said. Said.

Suad stared at a photograph of her late husband that was hanging on the wall next to her and silently called his name. She remembered the evening six months ago when she'd found him sitting on his favorite armchair; how she had seen the back of his head still and unmoving and how his black hair was peppered with streaks of gray, and how when she called out his name he didn't reply. He was still holding a needle in one hand and the yellow dress that he'd been putting the final touches to in the other.

Suad began stitching the arms and then the chest pieces and then the sides of Hilal's new suit.

"Threads are used by us tailors to connect pieces of cloth and to make an outfit—but invisible threads are used by God to knit people together. These invisible threads must never be cut in vain. How will we sew the broken pieces of our past back together? How will we bring all the separate parts into one whole? Tell me, Said, my darling, tell me," Suad asked her husband's photo. "Today, our son will come, and I'll finally tell him the truth."

At six o'clock that same evening, when Suad's doorbell rang it was not Hilal who stood at her door, but a girl with a large bush of curly light-brown hair, which framed her surprisingly cheeky face and bright green eyes. She was holding a small suitcase and looked as if she'd been on a long and arduous journey.

"Is Hilal here, Mrs. Shihab?' she asked.

"No," Suad said as her eyes fell on a second girl, who she had not noticed at first and who stood right behind the first one—a girl wearing a striking and most familiar yellow dress.

"Suha! *Suha!*" Suad called out and tried to put her arms around Suha, but Suha took a few steps back.

"I've waited for this moment all my life," Suad said to Suha with a shaking voice. "Oh, to see you in that dress, my beloved darling girl."

Suha touched Suad's arm gently as if to comfort her. "Perhaps there's a misunderstanding. I don't know you. You sent me this beautiful dress and I wanted to thank you, but who asked you to make it, who gave you my measurements, who paid for it? And what for?"

"No. No. No, it's not like that, it's not what you think. Of course *you* don't know me but I know you. Oh, Suha, Suha. No one ordered the dress from us, we sent it to you as a gift of love, as a distant embrace, and we hoped you might

142

one day come over and ask us about it. And I waited for you, I waited so long, and then I gave up all hope that you'd ever come."

"But if you wanted to talk to me, why didn't you just come and see me at home? Why send me a dress? Why play such games?" Suha said, and she looked at Suad as if she thought she had lost her marbles.

"I'll tell you the truth if you come in," Suad said in a trembling voice.

"What truth?" Suha asked her.

"The truth about you," Suad said.

Dunya looked at Suad, who was dressed in black from top to toe, and at Suha, whose yellow dress seemed to shimmer and shine in a way that couldn't be explained, neither by science nor by sense. And despite the differences between Suha and Suad—of age and dress and mood and attitude, it didn't take her long to guess what the truth was.

The lights were off in Suad's dark lounge, except for a tiny lamp in the corner. Some streetlight seeped in through the shutters. The floor was tiled with large, old-fashioned black and white tiles and the rest of the room was furnished sparsely, except for two old photographs in delicate wooden frames: one of Said and Suad on their wedding day; and the other of Hilal on his graduation day.

"Is this Hilal?" Suha pointed at Hilal's photograph with a shaking hand. "He does look like Nijm," she whispered in Dunya's ear. She took Dunya's hand in hers and sat next to her on a small sofa. She seemed afraid of what Suad was about to tell her.

"You were born here, my darling, *right here*." Suad pointed with a pale hand to a bedroom on the side of the lounge. "You came five minutes after your brother," she said.

Suad disclosed to both Suha and Dunya the *truth* in one long teary monologue without interruption, while Suha continued to hold Dunya's hand and Dunya dared to look at her only intermittently.

Where is Hilal? Where is Hilal, she kept thinking, and wishing she could run, run, run, run out of this house and out of this city, back to a time before she had found Suha.

The truth about Hilal and Suha was stranger than fiction, and had been covered up with a dark cloak of silence and lies—for reasons few would ever understand.

It was the year 1970, only a few days after the Corrective Movement Revolution which took place on March 8, when the recently wed Mr. and Mrs. Shihab moved into their marital nest and decided to transform it into a professional sewing atelier. The short man who delivered their two new Singer sewing machines said to them, "What an honor it must be for you to be the neighbors of Farida, Aleppo's most famous prophetess."

Mr. and Mrs. Shihab had never heard of Farida, but they soon discovered that their famous neighbor wasn't only a prophetess, but also the wife of Mustafa, the man who owned the soap shop downstairs and whose fragile ego was growing ever more fragile as he began to wake up to the fact that people were now visiting his shop not just to buy his excellent handmade bars of soap but to ask him for appointments to see his wife—thus forcing him to become her secretary.

Farida was celebrity number one in the mad souk of Aleppo. She was something like a grand mufti or even a pope in terms of her importance there. She told fortunes. Will you make a fortune? Will your child be fortunate? Or will your daughter have an unfortunate marriage? Who will marry and who will not, who will sinfully remarry or be unfaithful, who will have multiple wives or lives? Who will live and who will die?

In a country like Syria where there were so many secrets and where people lived in fear of the future and of the past, of what was hidden behind closed doors and round the corner, people could not live without professional secret-decoders. They were either the religious imams, who so often misguided people, or vagabonds and clairvoyants who always claimed to know the truth and to be able to read it either in coffee cups, the palms of hands, crystals, or by looking at people's auras. It was a very rare person in those days who had the courage to look for the truth in their own hearts. One of these rare people was Said, an unusual young man who found a tree leaf more interesting than the daily news of war and trade and who was a vehement non-believer in various subjects including the three official versions of God. To him bread was more important than God and love was more important than bread. Said knew that by only thinking this, he was joining a long line of heretics. The independent pursuit of truth had always been regarded as the ultimate act of arrogance and effrontery throughout every century, the most terrible profanity and the source of all blasphemy, the Original Sin committed by Adam at the instigation of Eve.

Suad and Said saw with their own eyes how people came to see their neighbor Farida from far and wide, but they were never tempted to join the queue. But over time Suad fell into a neighborly friendship with Farida, whom she soon discovered was an excellent cook. Farida, who was twice her age, taught Suad many of her traditional recipes, including her prized okra and lamb stew, and treated her like a daughter.

"You are pregnant, aren't you, my dear?" Farida asked Suad one day while they were chopping fresh parsley leaves together.

"No, I'm not," Suad said.

"Go and visit a doctor. I tell you, you are two months pregnant. I can see the beautiful soul entering your body; it's the soul of a poet. But perhaps it is two souls, possibly two poets. I will need to look into it further."

After a thorough medical investigation by the local doctor, Farida was proved right: Suad was indeed exactly two months pregnant.

The next day both Suad and Said gave in to their curiosity and requested a consultation with Farida in her professional capacity as a coffee-cup reader.

A round copper table with calligraphic religious text engraved on it, declaring *God is the Greatest*, carried a stack of letters and testimonials from all over the country sent in praise of Farida's unusual powers.

Said saw Farida's heavily mascaraed, big, black eyes and felt a tremor of fear. *Why are we doing this?* he wondered to himself.

A boy called Abdu came in holding an aluminum coffee jug. Silently and with much ceremony he poured the prophetic liquid into a porcelain cup and gravely handed it to Suad.

"Drink up," Farida said.

Suad did as she was told and after inverting the coffee cup over a saucer, and waiting for the sediments to grow into meaningful lines, Farida picked up the cup and started to read. She pursed her thin lips, and began trying to decipher the minutiae of Suad's coffee cup.

"You're about to have twins," she declared.

"Twins!" a gravelly man's voice could be heard muttering from behind the left wall.

"Is there someone eavesdropping on us?" Said asked.

"Don't worry," Farida whispered to her young visitors. "The cake maker and his wife often listen in, even though I've told them a hundred times not to. Unfortunately we have thin walls and we can't afford to change them. Neither prophecy nor soapmaking are lucrative enterprises. Anyway, you don't have to worry any more whether you'll be having a boy or a girl, because you'll in fact have both," she said.

"But we never worry about such things, Sitt Farida!" Suad said.

"The boy will be born first and then the girl."

Farida's expression began to change as she carefully inspected the sediments in her coffee cup.

"Tell me more," Suad asked her.

"There's nothing more to tell," Farida said rather glumly; a cloud suddenly appeared to be hovering over her wrinkled complexion.

After Suad had gone home, she wasn't able to forget what had happened. "Don't worry," Said told her. "Our neighbor is just the nervous type. She looks like the kind of woman who has hallucinations. Let's be happy. If she's right then we'll have everything we want, both a boy and a girl, and you won't have to suffer another pregnancy. And if she's wrong, well, that's only to be expected." Said kissed his wife on the nose. "Perhaps she guessed you were pregnant not because she's a prophetess but because, like most older women, she can read the usual signs. Don't be fooled, my treasure!"

But Suad couldn't sleep that night, or the night after.

If it weren't for Suad's insistence, Farida wouldn't have told her the unfortunate news she'd read in her coffee cup. But after Suad had a hormonally induced tear storm, Farida gave in to her request. "You don't have to believe me, my lovely, *but* what I saw in your cup was that if your boy and girl twins were to be kept together they would—they would. . . . Well, *it would not be good*."

"They would what? Tell me! Please don't hide the truth from me."

"Well, they—you will lose them both. . . . That is certain. I can see it behind the curtain. It is God's will."

Suad stood up in panic. "What do you mean, *I will lose them both*? What curtain? What do you mean, you are certain?"

"According to your coffee cup," Farida said, trying to look like a savant or a world-famous intellectual, "the boy must stay with you throughout his childhood, but you must give the girl away."

"What do you mean, *we must give the girl away*? How can I give my daughter up for no reason at all?" Suad said.

"All I can tell you is what I see in the cup."

"And the cup says I must give my daughter away?"

"Yes. That's what the cup says."

"How can I choose between a son and a daughter, just because a coffee cup says I must? Why would I believe a *cup*?"

"The cup does not say you can choose. You must keep your son." Farida raised one of her eyebrows as if she was beginning to lose patience. "No one is forcing you to believe the cup but if you don't, then don't say that I, or the cup, didn't warn you."

"Why are you lying to me like this? Can't you bear seeing a young couple happy?" Suad raised her voice at Farida.

"I'm just telling you what I've read in your coffee cup. If the cup has decided to lie, that's not my fault. I'm only a messenger."

"You're not a messenger. You're a liar. You should be ashamed of yourself, Farida." Suad ran out of the door.

Why did she come to see me in the first place if she thinks I'm a liar? People are so strange, Farida thought to herself and headed to the kitchen to put the final touches to her legendary dish of kibbeh.

Meanwhile gasps and giggles could clearly be heard from the cake shop next door. Instead of listening to the radio or watching TV while they made or sold cakes, the couple who owned the cake shop, an awful man and his awful wife, kept themselves entertained by doubling as professional eavesdroppers (it was a sort of job because it often paid).

In the beginning, Said and Suad didn't believe Farida and they stopped talking to her. But when (seven months later) Suad gave birth to twins, first a boy, then a girl, exactly as Farida had predicted, Said gravely walked down the stone steps and knocked on Farida's door.

"What shall we do, Sitt Farida?" he asked her.

"Who am I to say?" Farida said. "I'm a liar, after all, and I don't know what I'm talking about. I'm a bitter old woman who doesn't like to see young couples happy, aren't I? So why listen to me?"

"Please accept our apologies," Said said. "We were upset. We're young and naive. We dared to think we knew better than you."

"I forgive you," Farida said. "Let me ask around and see if there's a suitable family who might want to adopt your daughter. It needs to be the right family. Not just anyone will do."

The answer came within hours, from the cake maker and his wife, who knew of a respectable baker and his wife who lived on the opposite side of town who were desperately looking for a baby. Even though they naturally preferred a boy, a girl might do, they'd said—particularly now that Basma, the baker's wife, was in her ninth month of a heavy phantom pregnancy and had become sick and tired of wearing a duck-feather cushion inside a pair of extra-large red silk panties to dispel rumors about her infertility. Baker Bassam's snooty family, who were the cream of Aleppo's top baking dynasty, had threatened to disinherit him unless he produced an heir (or at the very least an heiress), very soon.

The next morning a one-day-old girl was promptly delivered to Bassam's bakery in what was possibly the most expensive breadbasket in history. This was because the cake maker had decided to make a fast lira, and he sold the baby girl to the bakers for an extortionate sum.

The only other thing that arrived in the breadbasket, apart from the baby, was a little note begging the new parents to call her Suha, a name that Said had always wanted his first daughter to be called because it was his mother's name and also because it was the name of a distant star of great beauty, whose light could not be seen by human eyes. What better name for a daughter whom he and his wife would, from that point, be forced to love from afar?

Suha listened intently to Suad's every word, but it was difficult to tell from the expression on her face how she felt about what she had heard. Dunya looked now and then at Suad's eyes and then at her shaking hands and her plain, dark, and rather tragic shoes, the shoes of a woman who has spent her entire life in the shade, where neither light nor dark pervade.

Despite the stark superficial differences between Suad and Suha, foisted upon them by age and circumstance, Dunya could see it as clear as day that Suad was the origin of Suha and that Suha was the hidden shadow she had seen so clearly in Hilal's face when she had first taken his photograph.

This was the girl she had asked him about and whom he denied existed.

The girl he had lost without his knowledge.

Suha sat next to Dunya, her hands still entwined in hers, on a small sofa opposite Suad, who sat alone in an armchair. It didn't seem strange that even though they'd only met that afternoon they were holding hands.

Dunya looked at Suha and she saw how she possessed Hilal's eyes, how her hair was like his, how her lips curved like his did, how her nose was shaped like his. And she looked at her coal black, almost blue hair and thought of the night and all the stars in it.

She could now feel Suha's hands shaking inside hers and knew that she was on the brink of tears. She could feel her shock at hearing the truth and the pain it caused rising in her like a storm. Dunya watched Suha as she stood up and flicked her hair away from her forehead. "Whether your story is true or false, Mrs. Shihab, I don't care. I already have a mother. No girl can have two mothers."

Suha picked up her handbag from the sofa, put her hand on Dunya's shoulder and leaned over and whispered in her ear, "Come and see me soon."

"I will," Dunya said.

She wanted to stand up and carry her traveling suitcase and follow Suha out of the door. It was hard for her to watch Suha disappear from sight.

"Suha," Suad called out. "Suha."

Every time she heard a noise at Suad's front door Dunya stood up hoping that it would be Hilal. But Hilal did not knock on his mother's door that night.

"I knew my son had found the woman who would complete him. I could see it on his face, in those photographs you sent us. I'm so happy to finally meet you in the flesh," Suad said. "But how on earth did you lose Hilal and then find Suha? It simply doesn't make sense."

"By accident," Dunya muttered. "Entirely by accident."

"No, it can't be an accident. Perhaps it was your fate to find her. Perhaps you will be the one who can bring sister back to brother. Will you help me do it?" Suad begged. "I need your help. Suha is so hurt and angry and as for Hilal, oh, he'll be too upset to speak to me ever again. He'll close his heart to me. That's what I'm afraid of, and then I'll lose them both . . . just as the coffee cup said."

"I will help you, Mrs. Shihab. And Hilal, first he will be upset but then he will understand. He will be so happy that Suha exists. It will change his life."

"Since he is so late, why don't you come and sleep in his bed," Suad took Dunya by the hand and led her to Hilal's bedroom. "I will put out a mattress in the lounge for him when he comes later."

Dunya spent her first night in Aleppo in Hilal's boyhood bed, holding his pillow to her chest. From the shutters of his bedroom window she looked at the rays of the moon as they touched his bedcover. But all she could think of was Suha.

Ever since she had known him, Dunya had felt it in her bones that Hilal possessed the ephemeral quality of moonlight and that there was something about him she could not quite hold onto, and she had even occasionally imagined that one day if she blinked or if she turned her gaze away from him, when she looked back again she wouldn't find him, and that she'd discover he was nothing but a beautiful dream she'd woven for herself, or a wonderful whimsy. Might she not one day lose him, the way another girl might lose her hat or scarf in a windstorm, or at sea? She'd imagined those unlikely scenarios, but it had never occurred to her that it would happen another way and that what she would one day lose was not Hilal but the certainty of her love for him, her certainty that he was the only One. That certainty and that feeling of eternity she didn't lose in an afternoon breeze but during an unexpected and intense summer storm, which took place silently while she drank a glass of freshly made lemonade.

Early the next morning a boy who was no taller than 136 centimeters knocked on Mrs Shihab's door and delivered to her the following letter which was folded inside a dirty brown envelope:

SYRIAN ARMY CENTRAL CONSCRIPTION UNIT
LONG LIVE THE HOMELAND
8-6-1996. Ref. HC001
Dear Mrs. Suad Shihab,
I am writing on behalf of your son, Hilal Said Shihab, who has requested that we inform you of his decision to join our noble National Army in order to defend the homeland.

Your son will contact you once he has successfully completed our four-year world-famous Elite Brigade induction program.

Meanwhile, any attempts by you or your family to contact him will be deemed highly unpatriotic and will incur grave consequences.

Yours Truly,
Lieutenant-in-Chief QASEM BAKR AL-SHUGHOUR
Central Army Conscription Unit
The Democratic Republic of Syria.

BOOK FOUR
The Lessons of Love

If 1 + 1 = True Love, what is 1 + 2 equal to?

18

A Father's Advice

A PHOTOGRAPH OF DUNYA AS a little girl standing in front of her father took pride of place on the Noors' mantelpiece. Joseph had one of his hands playfully in her curls. He looked so big in his stripy suit and she so small. Her curly hair reached up to his heart, even though she was only as high as his belly.

"You must help him, Dad, please?" Dunya said to Joseph. "I'm just a young woman who nobody knows and Hilal's mother's a simple seamstress and a widow, if we go to the army asking for an explanation they'll jeer at us and shoo us out of their offices. But they can't do that to you."

"There's no difference in our country between a doctor and a seamstress, or a young girl like you. We're all equal in the eyes of the revolution." Joseph flicked a stray hair off his forehead and looked sternly at Dunya. "If it's true he's in the army, all I can say is the army could yet make a man of him," he continued in a steady voice and took a sip of water from a glass nearby. "But I don't believe it," he stated in an imperious tone. "This letter, let's face it, is nonsense. I bet you Hilal paid someone to type it for him and get it promptly delivered, and now he's off somewhere proposing marriage to another girl. What tricks these boys get up to satisfy their endless pride! The army doesn't write letters like that and neither do they need mummy's boys like Hilal."

"Hilal would never play such tricks, Dad, never. Can't you ask one of your friends at the Baath Party to contact the lieutenant who wrote that letter and ask him about it?"

"What?" Joseph laughed. "Do you think we're in Surrey or in Hampshire, my dear Dunya, and that the army and the Baath party are the local Citizen's Advice Bureau? Wake up from your afternoon snooze, darling. I told you I'm an expert judge of character. And a man like that Hilal boy, who dedicates his scientific career to the study of moonlight, is perfectly capable of a cowardly disappearing act. A boy of that sort is nothing but starry-eyed moonshine, a master of fairy-tales and airy nonsense. His feelings are like soap bubbles," Joseph said. "As you know, my darling, I'm a very busy man. How would the Joseph Noor Heart Foundation run if I spent my time running around on wild goosechases? I need to draw the line somewhere."

Dunya could see it very clearly: Joseph was positively delighted now that Hilal was out of the picture and he wasn't going to lift a finger to help her find him. If only he knew that it was not Hilal who was fickle, feckless, insincere, and a hypocrite and whose feelings were like soap bubbles. It was she, his daughter, who was like that. It was not Hilal whose love couldn't be counted on or trusted, it was *her* love. Dunya looked down at the floor in shame, giving Joseph completely the wrong impression. He now imagined that he had won his battle.

Patricia held Dunya in her arms and whispered in her ears, "Stop insisting, darling, it'll only make him more stubborn. Go and see Mr. Ghazi, I'm sure he has contacts, too. Your father's not the only well-connected man in Latakia, even though he thinks he is." She looked at Joseph with heavy-lidded eyes. "You're a cruel man," her eyes seemed to say. "You're a cold-hearted father."

"You need so much guidance and protection, my little curly haired sparrow. I just wish you knew how much," Joseph said to Dunya in a gentle voice, when he saw how her tears fell, how she sat on a little armchair alone with her curls between her palms, hiding her face in what he did not know was shame. He tried not to feel a little pang of guilt and a little sorrow for her. She was his only daughter, his only child, she was his small and rather tragic sparrow, the only human being who was his—well, except for Patricia.

Mr. Ghazi had often thought to himself that the ownership of an entire hospital and a summer home could not override the damage done to poor Joseph's social standing by fathering a daughter like Dunya. But then again, in the flesh she was so charming, almost disarming.

Mrs. Ghazi was wearing a black and white polka-dot dress and was looking at Dunya with x-ray eyes. She had her hair in rollers and a long cigarette hung from her plum-colored mouth. A large, framed, fake Mona Lisa, smiling her usual unnerving smile, hung on the wall opposite, and next to it there was a large photograph of a young man in a suit with a rather smug look on his face and a couple of glassy skyscrapers behind him. "This must be George," Dunya said.

"He's handsome, isn't he?" Mrs Ghazi said to Dunya with a clear undertone of "You can look but you can't touch."

"He's not only handsome, he's so much more than that. In fact, he's a prize to be won and every single young woman who meets him dreams he might one day be her husband. Duels are expected in his honor when he returns to Latakia next week," Mr. Ghazi bragged.

"You could have him if you want to, Dunya. . . ." he added casually.

"*She* could have him?" Mrs Ghazi said with alarm. "Says who?" She glared at her husband Salman.

But he continued to look at Dunya with a gentle expectation in his eyes.

Dunya stared at Mr. Ghazi and his wife and wondered what the most polite thing to say would be. How to refuse without causing mortal offense? For the consequences of displeasing the Ghazis could not be foretold.

"George is coming to Latakia next week and he specifically asked to see you, Dunya. When he heard you were back in town he was beside himself with joy," Mr. Ghazi said. "Didn't Maria tell you?"

"No," Dunya said.

"He always had a soft spot for you and when you left to England so suddenly, he was heartbroken," he claimed.

"That's very touching, Mr. Ghazi, but I'm already in love with someone else. Love is not a matter of choice don't you agree?" Dunya said.

"Says who?" Mr. Ghazi said suspiciously. "You girls have strange ideas about love, frankly rather out-of-date ideas, most unfashionable."

"In any case, I've already promised George's hand to my niece. Dunya is too modern for our George," Mrs. Ghazi said defensively. "George needs an old-fashioned wife who can cook him all the dishes I make and who does as she's told. Can you say you could be such a wife, Dunya?"

"No," Dunya said.

"Well, I didn't think so," Mrs. Ghazi said as if this had settled the matter.

Clearly Mr. Ghazi had not yet updated his wife about his little chat with Joseph. If George married Dunya, the mother of their grandchildren would not be a virgin, admittedly. Ghazi gritted his teeth. It would be a huge sacrifice of course. But as a Christian, he was familiar with the concept of sacrifice. Everyone knew that the minute Dunya left Syria unchaperoned by a Syrian adult, albeit at the tender age of thirteen, her moral status and therefore marriageability had become suspect. Everyone in Latakia was convinced she must have lost her morals minutes after landing in London and that every moment of her life there was spent in a further state of moral decrepitude and physical undress. In London the temptations were too strong and the restrictions nonexistent and so who in their right mind would be able to resist them? That was what people reasoned in Lattakia. And they had also heard from various trusted sources that in the western world being a virgin was not regarded as a source of social status, as in Syria, but the very opposite. It was a stigma that every teenager was encouraged to get rid of as soon as they possibly could. Rumors circulating about her spending her first night back in Latakia in a cheap two-star hotel with a long-haired stranger only proved that rather sore point. But if George married Dunya, Mr. Ghazi reasoned, he would inherit the Joseph Noor Heart Foundation, which was worth at least ten million dollars. Future profits were sure to be phenomenal, what with the rate of heart attacks that were sweeping the country, thanks to the economy doing so badly and the dodgy political situation, not to mention the escalating number of scandals and elopements (the rate of daughters eloping with unwanted men had quadrupled in the last five years alone). It was a traumatic time for many fathers, Mr. Ghazi thought to himself. In the same breath, he praised the Lord that Maria was such a good girl.

"All girls are the same, none of them are different. Not even Dunya," Mr. Ghazi lectured. "No girl can have a destiny without the right man by her side. This is nature's law, my darling, and you must accept your place in it. Dunya's problem is that she thinks she can change the world, and people like that always end up unhappy. You know the type, the bitter spinsters who live with their cats or in lonely contemplation of their collection of hats. Nothing is sadder than a woman who's lost her way. This is where a father's role comes in and why his guidance is indispensable. Girls follow their hearts, the most deceiving instrument that God has given womankind."

"I smell a rat," Maria said later when they were alone in her room, where the French doors were open onto a balcony with views of the sea. She'd reread the Syrian Army letter for the third time. "This clearly isn't a normal conscription unit, it sounds more like a citizens' kidnapping unit. My advice to you, Dunya, is to skilfully pretend to your father and mine that you've given up looking for Hilal and that you're considering George as an alternative spouse."

"No way!"

"Of course you won't give up on Hilal, you'll simply *pretend*. It's not as difficult to do as you think. I can teach you. Meanwhile, I know the man who can help you, Dunya, if I ask him to," Maria said in a proud tone. "I too have contacts, you know."

"Do you mean your fiancé Shadi?" Dunya said.

"Of course not Shadi. We must keep this a secret, especially from Shadi," Maria said under her breath. "I don't even like Shadi."

"You don't like Shadi?" Dunya looked surprised.

"Shadi has a major flaw," Maria said calmly. "He's too perfect, you see. My mother is in love with him and my father is too. He flirts more with them than with me and he often acts as if he's about to marry them. In return, I'm also expected to flirt with his parents, and I'm already thoroughly bored of it, but I have no choice except to marry him. I must marry Shadi," Maria said as if she was trying to convince herself of the inevitability of having a wisdom tooth extracted or a similarly unpleasant but necessary operation.

"But why must you marry Shadi?" Dunya asked her. "Why not wait until you fall in love with someone and then marry that person? What's the hurry?"

Maria stood up and looked out of her window onto the street below. She hid her face between her hands and said, "I'm already in love, Dunya, desperately in love with a man I cannot have." Tears began to slide down Maria's cheeks. "So I might as well marry Shadi and be done with it."

"You are already in love?" Dunya said. "But with a man you cannot have?"

"Hush! Keep your voice down." Maria put her hand over Dunya's mouth. "His name is Mr. Saddiq," she whispered.

"He's twenty-eight years older than me, two inches shorter than me when I'm not wearing any heels, and . . . he has a large rotund belly any belly dancer would be proud of. So there, I said it."

"Oh," Dunya said. "Well, so what? If you love him so much why care about his big belly and his being so much older and shorter, that's no reason not to marry him Maria, is it?"

"Well, there's more bad news Dunya. First of all he's also a senior Baath party official and an Alawite from the village of Kurdaha, as well as being a father of six and husband to one."

"Oh," Dunya now understood. Falling in love with a Baath party official, now that was the limit. And a married one at that.

"He just fell into his job," Maria said, shamefaced. "Family connections. He doesn't take any of it seriously."

Everything about Mr. Saddiq was wrong, each one of his qualities and each of his circumstances was utterly, utterly wrong. Even a girl as rebellious as Dunya disapproved. *Maria is in love with a senior Baath Party official? "How could you?"* she wanted to say, *"How could you fall in love with one of them, a criminal and a crook?"* But she didn't. What moral authority did she have when her own heart had led her astray too, and only yesterday? Perhaps Mr. Ghazi was right after all, perhaps the heart is a dangerous instrument and one should not always blindly listen to it, or follow its dangerous dictates.

"Anyway," Maria said. "So even though Saddiq was put on this earth to break my heart, and I his, he's the man who'll get Hilal back for you. I promise you he can do it without even breaking into a sweat."

"You think so?" Dunya said. "It does seem lucky for Hilal and I that you fell in love with one of *them*—in the circumstances. But are you sure he is not corrupt?" Dunya couldn't resist asking.

"He's not corrupt, no, no, I promise you." Maria put her arms around Dunya.

Love is blind, Dunya thought to herself, *but what is most important now is for her to get Hilal out of the Syrian Army's clutches and then promptly fall back in love with him—and only him.*

That evening Dunya stood alone on her bedroom balcony and vowed to herself and to the sky and to the night that she would put a veil over her love for Suha, and that she would never mention her name, nor ever think of her, that she would only think of Hilal, and slowly, slowly Suha would disappear back to where she'd always been—the world of shadows and of dreams.

19

The Baker's Unreal Daughter

SUHA HABIBI HAD ALWAYS BELIEVED that she was the only, and rather spoiled, daughter of Basma Habibi, a former mawaal singer who lived in the northern suburbs of Aleppo, and Bassam Habibi, a reputable baker who died a couple of years ago under a collapsed building, which fell on him like a pack of cards after a Turkish earthquake sent a few of its terrible tremors all the way to Aleppo.

But even as a child it was difficult for her to ignore the fact that she didn't seem to have inherited any of the physical or psychological characteristics of either of her two doting parents. She looked very hard and often but she could not find an eyelash, a finger, an ankle, a smile, let alone a nose in common with either of them. Even though she had always been told that Basma, 'the Rose of Aleppo,' was her mother, Suha often looked at Basma and irrationally thought, *This is not how I'd imagine my mother to be*. What a strange thought that was, and that is why she hid it well. And though she had a continuous itchy feeling of undaughterliness toward them, she never suspected what the real reason was. Neither did she understand why she felt puzzled most of the time. And then one day, perhaps when she was twelve, she overheard someone say that Basma was, "more famous for being barren than for her singing." As soon as she heard this, she wiped it out of her consciousness, and refused to contemplate it. Instead, she intensified her efforts to appear daughterly.

From the moment she was born and all throughout her childhood and youth, everyone around Suha intended to keep her in the dark. She had never lacked for anything except for truth. Was this perhaps why her hair was so dark? But then again, so many women's hair around there was darker than the darkest night.

Suha had learned early on how to be secretive. Everything in her life with Bassam and Basma often took on the air of pretense and of make-believe. Basma had lied to her and to the world so much that in the end Suha didn't have a clue any more what was what, who was who and what to do. Basma lied purely because she didn't want the truth to be true. And so, although Suha was an actress by temperament, it was also forced on her through upbringing; it was a conspiracy of both nature and time. Very early on in her life she wanted to find a story or a song that might explain the world to her. She had always suspected that words might be like keys and sentences like doorways.

The first time Suha heard Basma singing she thought it was the radio. The song was so beautiful that it made her heart beat faster than it had ever done before. As she followed the song to its source she realized that it wasn't coming out of the radio, but that it was her mother who was singing it. She saw her in their living room holding an oud in her hands. She could not at first understand why her mother had never sung in front of her before, but she didn't ask her why then, and instead she took her mother's oud into her hands and tried to play it. The sound that came out was most unpleasant and jarring on the ears. Then, when Suha tried to copy her mother's singing, Basma looked at her with wide-open eyes:

Oh night, oh night,
Light of my eyes,
My heart and my soul
Are longing for you!

The sound of Suha's voice filled the room.

"Your voice." her mother said in alarm.

"What about my voice?" Suha asked her.

"It is . . . it is like no other voice I have ever heard," Basma whispered with fear.

Oh night, oh night,
In the sky above,
My heart soars
Looking for you . . .
The night, the night . . .
Is hiding you from me!
The night, the night
Is hiding me from you!

"Why are you doing this to me, God? Is this my punishment, are you testing me?" Basma said.

Suha sang louder and louder and as she heard her own voice for the first time, she suddenly and unexpectedly discovered the purpose and meaning of her life. As she gradually allowed her song to soar she no longer felt lost. Everything was filled with luminosity and meaning. Her whole body and her heart and mind were filled with an extraordinary sensation she had never known until that day. She continued to sing, improvising new words and tunes and remembering songs she'd heard before, her heart sprang to life and its beats filled her whole being until tears began flowing from her eyes.

It was then that she realized that her voice could express so much of what had previously been hidden from her as a little girl. A little girl who was in the habit of hiding from the world and fearful of asking questions whose answers she never dreamed she would discover.

Song was her answer; it filled her world with the beginning of meaning, and a strange delightful feeling that was so much bigger than her, and larger than her world.

"Hush!" Basma said. "Stop, stop!" And she went and locked the door and closed the windows.

"I'm like you, I'm like you. I can sing like you." Suha shouted with joy and jumped up and down and ran in circles around her mother and then put her arms around her.

"My darling, you're not like me, you're much better than me," Basma said gently but in a very sad voice. "I don't want you to sing. It's the worst destiny to be born into. The love of music is a curse."

"How did you make that oud sing? I want you to show me." Suha stubbornly ignored her mother's words.

"I can't do that," Basma said. "Your father will kill us both."

"Why?" Suha said.

"When he married me, he made me promise to give music up, and the last thing he'd want is for me to teach it to you. Most men are not like your father and you'll never find a husband if you sing. No respectable man wants to marry a songbird."

Suha begged Basma every day for more than a year to teach her the oud and she threw a number of tantrums, until in the end Basma gave in. "But you must promise me not to sing in front of anyone, ever. And you must never nurture a dream of becoming a professional singer. Promise me, my love."

"I promise," Suha said.

"If only one could sing silently then we could do it all day and all night and no one would be able to stop us . . . then we would be happy, wouldn't we, my dove?" Basma sometimes said wistfully, observing how happy they both were when they let themselves sing to their heart's content.

"Why are Fairuz and Umm Kulthoum allowed to sing in public and we're not?" Suha sometimes asked her mother.

"How should I know?" Basma always answered.

By keeping the secret of her beautiful voice hidden, and not being allowed to display it, Suha often felt as if she was about to explode. She wished she could scream it out from the rooftops, "I am a singer! I am a singer! Listen to my song!"

But she never did.

Neither did she dare to declare that her love of the oud was absolute.

Over the years Basma taught Suha how to hide her musical talent the way others hid their sins and misfortunes. But she also secretly taught her how to sing like Asmahan and play the oud like Farid al-Atrash.

But as Suha grew, her parents' insecurities also grew. And the only way for them to deal with their fears was to work harder and harder to forget about Suha's past, and they became utterly obsessed with her future. As she was so beautiful, they never had a doubt that she would be able to pick and choose in the husband department, but that was not enough for them. They also wanted her to have a career. They had heard that many women were now becoming professionals. That there were women who were architects, lawyers, engineers, doctors. Doctors! That last one took their fancy. In no time they started to pressure Suha to develop at least a pretense of wanting to become a doctor. However, in reality they knew and she knew that this was the last thing she wanted. But any indication of her indifference to a medical career would automatically push Basma over the edge. "I don't want you to have anything to do with music, look what happened to me. I'm a shadow of my former self. Any profession rooted in emotion and fantasy can only suck a person dry and in the end, kill them. Be a doctor. Get respect." That is what Basma said more than once to Suha, while nervously gritting her teeth of gold. Half of Basma's teeth were twenty-one carat gold, because it was fashionable for middle-aged women in those days. (It also ensured financial security if divorced or widowed, or in old age, as the gold teeth could be sold and replaced with porcelain ones in times of need.)

So, Suha pretended she was planning to study medicine, perhaps one day. But, she spent as much time as possible learning how to play the oud from Basma, who knew everything there was to know about it. They did that in secret, as Bassam's family would have been outraged to hear that Basma was teaching her daughter such whorish arts.

By the time Suha reached the ripe age of eighteen her stock as a 'prize-bride' was rapidly rising and word spread far and wide about the perfection of her lips, the impossible silkiness of her long, black hair and her amazingly seductive and hypnotic eyes. Bride-hunters, who hunted on behalf of their sons, brothers, and cousins, spoke of her skin and her limbs, her melodious voice and her body, which seemed to be full of fire and light and a heat—all impossible to describe and in no time people came to Suha's father hoping that they could win her hand (as well as her heart). They brought rings and necklaces with them, jewelry and pastries; they listed their accomplishments and possessions and boasted of their virtues both real and imaginary. Her hopeful grooms were rumored to include a bulging doctor, a cacophonous lawyer, a not-unattractive merchant, and a dentist from Damascus. For a daughter of a baker this was quite an achievement. Dentist Karim was Suha's most eligible suitor. His hair was dark brown, his shoulders square. His jaw was also square, but his eyes were not; they were almond-shaped and a dark mahogany color. He often wore a beige cotton suit with a white shirt and was always clean-shaven. He had thick, well-combed, fragrant hair, while his eyebrows were so neatly arched that Suha wondered whether he occasionally plucked them. His story with Suha is a long one and sadly does not fit in this book.

There was no way that Basma's father would give her in marriage to anyone who could not provide her with a certain lifestyle, a life of luxury and social status. It was through his daughter, Suha, that Bassam the baker had decided his family would finally be able to rise meteorically into the social stratosphere. Yes, Suha was his daughter and he loved her, but like most good daughters she was also an asset, worth her weight in gold.

But one suitor after another, she refused. None of the men who proposed to her seemed anywhere near alluring to her. She hated the idea of being married off to some stranger who would then think he owned her.

She wanted to sing! She wanted to sing, sing, sing. And she wanted to love, really love, someone who truly loved her the way she wanted to be loved. She didn't want jewelry or houses, nor did she want to hear of her prospective grooms' portfolio of accomplishments and successes. No, she wanted so much more than that. How could she sell her love to the highest bidder? This was not what love was all about. She wanted something far more precious than that, something that the world had clearly given up on and considered worthless. Unlike many other girls in the neighborhood, Suha knew for sure that she was not the equivalent of a washing machine or of the latest Ferrari, and she insisted that it was her heart that must choose the one that she would love. Her heart must choose, and it would not be chosen. It must give and it would not be given.

Until she could find her way out of this impossible conundrum, Suha was busy being a rather lazy student at the Faculty of Philosophy at Aleppo University, as well as a famous heartbreaker and flirt, and she continued to promise her mother that one day she would be a doctor, though what kind of doctor this was, Basma never understood.

"A doctor of philosophy!" Suha explained.

Then one day a yellow dress arrived at Mr. and Mrs. Habibi's doorstep, wrapped loosely in the day's edition of the *al-Thawra* newspaper (published by the Baath Party and a source of all essential truth and bulletproof fact). Suha had been sipping tea with her mother on the balcony when she heard the bell ringing and then found that parcel waiting for her at the door. When she tried the dress on, Suha was sur-prised to discover that it fit her perfectly, every line and every curve. And not only that, but she also noticed when she looked at herself in the mirror (as did her mother) that the yellow dress, which seemed to hold her gently and softly, had the effect of a ray of sun when it shines into an area of shadow.

At first Basma was convinced that it was one of Suha's many admirers who had sent that dress to her as a present, but after she inspected it carefully and read its label, she violently threw the dress on the floor as if it were about to burn her. "I'll put it away in the loft, don't ever wear it again," she said to Suha as she tried to pick up the dress quickly from the floor. But Suha got there first. "Of course I'm going to wear it. Why shouldn't I wear it? It's the most beautiful dress I've ever had."

Suha read its label.

Exclusively Made by Said & Suad Shihab, His & Hers Sew-ing Atelier, Aleppo

"I know that atelier," she said. "Maybe we could ask them who ordered the dress from them, and then we'll know who it was."

"No! Don't ever go and see them. Don't ever ask them anything! Do you hear me?" Basma said gravely.

"But why not, Mother?" Suha said.

"No whys and no buts. Don't ever go to see them, don't ever speak to them, don't ever have anything to do with them. And if you do . . ." Basma said in a tragic and doom-laden voice.

"If I do, what?"

"If you do then I'll no longer be your mother," she threatened.

Things were always either black or white with Basma, and her life had not helped her understand or accept the possibili-ties in between. Suha knew that she must not question her openly or imagine that she could ever discuss things or argue with her, she knew that it was *so* and only so with Basma, whose life had made it difficult for her to be any other way, but Suha loved her and she never wanted to lose her. She loved her fearful mother Basma.

It was now the middle of June, a lazy summer's afternoon. Suha sat in a wicker chair opposite her bed and rested her legs over the bedsheets, one over the other. Her bedroom was on the fourth floor, as high as the top of a palm tree whose leaves touched her windowpane. In one of her hands she held an old book of love poems by the dreamy and cheeky and erotic Syrian poet Nizar al-Qabbani. It was so hot even the air blown from the electric fan whirring away on a table beside her was not enough. So, when were Dunya and Hilal finally going to come and find her? She'd been waiting for days and refused to go out while waiting for them. Waiting and waiting.

These two had come into her life so suddenly and unexpectedly, and everything seemed so different now. She needed hours and days and all night to think about it, to try to understand. What did it all mean? The truth had finally come to her in the unexpected shape of a girl who, when she first met her, imagined her to be a boy. This truth was so outlandish that it had turned her life upside down. Her thoughts, her feelings, her beliefs, her world had been broken—light had been shone into the darkness. But she still could not see.

Dunya had come into her life and with her the truth had also come. In addition to a new mother, a new brother, a new sense of who she was and who she might become, Dunya had innocently smiled at her, had uttered strange and unexpected words, and carried her camera in her hands like a torch with which she lit her world.

Suha had never met a girl like Dunya, nor imagined that she existed, and now that she had met her, everything seemed different. Many things that she thought were impossible now seemed possible, even inevitable. *Dunya*, her name rang in her ears, and she played back in her mind that moment Dunya came and spoke to her. She played it back to herself like an old movie, moment by moment from beginning to end, and imagined the sequel. What would happen next?

Suha fanned herself with a paper fan now and then and continued to read poem after poem to kill the minutes and hours and days while she waited, and to distract herself from thinking about Dunya. And Hilal. The two of them were bound to come and see her. Suha waited, and waited, every minute weighing on her like an hour, every hour like a historical age. She turned page after page of her book of poems, none of which she could read, because all she could see in front of her, and on each line of those pages, was Dunya's face, followed soon after by what she imagined Hilal might look like. All she could hear inside her ears were words that Dunya had said, interrupted by the sounds of traffic and shouting from the streets below.

What type of man, Suha wondered, *was Hilal?* Was he like her? Was she anything like him? Even though they had such different lives, and he was a boy, there must be something in their core that was one and the same, because he was her twin and she had known him before they were born. Might he love her as his sister, might she love him as her brother? Would they be drawn to one another or would they be indifferent?

Suha remembered how as a little girl she had sometimes wished that she had had a brother or even a sister. She'd always carried an imaginary image of a sibling in her heart. Did she want a brother? An actual, real brother? This real one might be different from the one she'd carried inside her. This real one was the one she'd been thrown away in favor of. From the moment they were born he'd been the first, and she the last. He was the one who was chosen and lived in the light, while she was rejected and exiled to the dark. Everything since then and after had been his.

Everything she wanted.

*

Suha got up from her armchair and brought over her portable cassette player. She picked out from her bookcase a tape whose cover was a black-and-white photograph of a melancholy young man with a beautiful face, pitch-black straight hair, and a side parting. His name: Abdel-Halim Hafez.

She pressed the play button.

> She sat. She sat, and there was sadness in her eyes,
> Staring at my turned-up coffee cup.
> She said: My boy, don't be sad.
> My boy, don't be sad, for love is your destiny.
> Love is your destiny.
> I have gazed into the future, many times. I have looked
> into the stars.
> But I've never read a coffee cup like yours before.
> I've never known a sadness like yours before,
> My boy, my boy!

It was upon first hearing that particular song that Suha had been reminded, through its lyrics and its rhymes and the heartbreaking voice of its legendary orphan-boy singer, that there was something in the world that she wanted with all her heart to reach and to touch and to hold, and that it was *love* in its purest, truest sense. But although Abdel-Halim sang about the tragic impossibility of such a pursuit, she had decided that she, unlike the hero of this song, would find it, and that she would not listen to anyone else's nonsense about the impossibility of such a pursuit and would summon up the boldness to hold it in her hand like a beautiful bird whose soul was her destiny.

Unlike the doom-laden and eternally heartbroken hero of that song, Suha was determined that she would not live a life of living death, and that unlike him and many others like him she would choose to live, live, live.

175

*

The next day Dunya arrived at the Aleppo Central Bakery early in the morning.

First, she knocked at the hakawati's door, but no one answered, and then she summoned up the courage to ask the two young men who were running the Aleppo Central Bakery whether they knew who Suha Habibi was and her whereabouts.

Suha was sitting at her desk pretending to study when she heard her cousin Badri calling her. Then she heard her other cousin Aziz knocking on the door. "A curly haired girl is here to see you," he told her.

Suha ran with him down the stairs, forgetting to put on her slippers or any shoes.

After Suha's father Baker Bassam died, Badri and Aziz, both of whom were as tall as trees (about two meters each to be exact), took over his bakery. They redecorated it, painting it white all over, and employed a team of ten young boys to deliver bread on antiquated bicycles to all the restaurants in Aleppo, and sometimes sweep the floors and make teas and coffees. Badri and Aziz also had a van and a wife each, as well as a tribe of children whose names they could hardly remember as they worked too hard to focus on such trivialities.

In a backroom full of bags of flour that had been laid one on top of the other, the length and breadth of three of the walls, Suha found Dunya standing between her two tall and burly cousins, both of whom were dressed in their usual jeans and vests, exposing their large hairy chests and wide, manly shoulders.

The first thing she noticed was how tiny Dunya appeared in comparison to them, and then how her curls, which had seemed so wildly playful and cheeky and romantic and full of rays of an invisible golden sun, seemed to be sorrowful today.

And then there were Dunya's eyes, which she looked at, and which instead of looking at her with delight seemed to be hiding behind a sort of cloud. Dunya's eyes were so different; it was as if summer had turned to winter inside them, as if the ray of love and sun and happiness that shone through them had been extinguished.

"Dunya?" Suha grabbed her hands. "What happened?"

Dunya looked at Suha's face for a moment. She didn't dare to look in her eyes, so she looked instead at her cheeks, at her chin, then gave up and buried her face in her hair, putting her arms around her chest and holding her very tightly. "Oh Suha, Suha."

The two of them stood like that for a moment or two while Suha's two cousins watched them with raised eyebrows.

"I wanted to bring Hilal to see you," Dunya said in a soft voice. "But he did not come home that night, and the next morning a boy delivered a letter . . ."

(Of course, Dunya made sure not to mention Hilal's link to Suha in front of her cousins.)

With a sharp, long whistle Aziz summoned a teenage boy who was lingering in the corner. "Jamal! Go and buy a big chocolate gateau for our lovely lady guest. Take the bicycle, Jamal."

"Hamoudi," he called out to another boy, "four teas please."

Dunya explained to Suha, Aziz, and Badri how her sweetheart Hilal had been snatched by the Syrian Army from his hotel in Latakia, and how they had sent his mother a highly suspicious, typed letter. The four of them spent an hour or so slowly sipping their sugared teas, concocting strategies, weighing options, and baking up a cunning plan around a wooden table.

As Suha's cousins (both ex-Syrian army conscripts) offered their expert advice, Dunya tried to keep her eyes and thoughts away from Suha. But Suha was sitting next to her on a wooden bench and she kept accidentally moving nearer and nearer until in the end she was almost glued to Dunya's side. Every time Dunya moved toward the far edge of the seat, Suha would follow her like a cat. Then, in the end, the two sat side by side on one half of the bench and Suha put one of her arms around Dunya.

Suha's touch distracted Dunya and she had to concentrate hard to hear what the cousins were saying. How she longed to put her arms around Suha too and to sit with her alone and just stare at her. She simply wanted to stare at her. Take her in. Who *was* this girl? The mystery of her, the strong impact her presence had on Dunya was something she still could not understand, or accept. Suha was so carefree and unselfconscious and she held her tightly and without shame, perhaps because she did not feel that there was anything to feel ashamed about. But she, Dunya, felt almost paralyzed by fear and shame for the first time in her life.

For the last three days she hadn't been able to sleep. Whether her eyes were open or shut all she could see was Suha. When she tried to brush her hair, there Suha was between the brush and her hair. When she tried to put a spoon of yogurt in her mouth, there was Suha, between the spoon and her lips. She could taste her. When she dressed she felt Suha between her clothes and her skin. Suha was suddenly all around her, inside and outside her. When Dunya looked out of the window, she saw Suha. Suha was always there. And here she was now, painfully real, sitting next to her, no longer floating in her dreams at a safe distance.

Suha wore a sky-blue dress, her feet were bare and they dangled from the bench, she had her arms around Dunya, her fingers occasionally affectionately brushing her hair. This made Dunya feel so nervous that she could hardly breathe. As the cousins spoke and made suggestions, Dunya could feel both Suha and Hilal battling inside her heart, but it was clear to her who had won, and who had dethroned the other. Suha won without doing a thing, without lifting a finger, without knowing, or wanting to. She'd won Dunya's heart, but what, then, was she going to do with it?

Dunya wished she could cover herself with a large bag, so that Suha would not be able to see her, nor guess at how she felt and what she wanted.

"Hey, cheer up, Dunya," Suha said to her. "We'll find Hilal, you and me. It's nothing but a tempest in a teapot." She took one of Dunya's longer curls and rolled it around her finger. "Don't worry those pretty curls," she said. "I much preferred you when you were more silly, not so serious. Come on, smile, smile, be reckless, be feckless, like you were before. Don't frown like this, it doesn't suit you. My cousins will take care of Hilal, won't you, boys?"

"Yeah," Aziz said. "Suha is right, don't worry, Miss. My advice is to start by trying to find out where exactly Hilal is stationed. In the beginning we must rule out the obvious possibilities, for example, there's a large barracks outside Aleppo. Could he not be there? He's an Aleppo boy after all and that's where Badri and I were stationed when we first started our army service, before we were sent out to other units. I know people who work there, cleaners, bread-delivery boys, low-level contacts, but it's better than nothing, no?"

"No?" Dunya said. "Oh yes, yes, I mean yes. Well, why can't we simply drive up to the Aleppo barracks and ask them if Hilal is there, and then we'll have our answer?"

"No!" Aziz panicked. "Please don't try that!"

"Why not?" Dunya asked.

Suha playfully slapped Dunya's cheeks on both sides. "Why not? Indeed, why not? Tell that silly girl, Aziz, why not?" she said.

"Because—well, Miss Dunya, your fiancé hasn't been recruited in the conventional way, obviously, he's in some sort of trouble, isn't he? If we draw attention to ourselves, we might get tarred with the same brush as him. We men could get beaten up, whipped. You girls, well, we can't be sending girls to army barracks, now can we?" Aziz scratched his head. "We need a roundabout way of doing it."

Dunya found out more about Suha's charming cousins over bites of the delicious cake that eventually arrived in a cardboard box. Their tall, strong physiques, developed over years of carrying bags of flour across their shoulders and kneading bread fast and furiously, were ideal for the job, where apart from making bread they often had to stand between customers when fights broke out. This happened quite regularly, according to Badri and Aziz, because often when a woman came in unaccompanied she would get her bottom pinched, and then all hell would break loose. The woman would start screaming and then she would violently slap the first man she saw or hit him with her handbag. The men would start beating each other up, loaves of bread would fly, and so on. Sometimes men—of the tough and hardened variety, known locally as zeeraans—would untie their belts, pull them out, and start whipping the air or anyone they could catch.

As the cousins told their colorful stories to Dunya, Suha looked at her and every now and then she touched her hand, or her cheek, or her foot playfully; it was as if she was trying her hardest to bring back the girl she had met on the first day before Dunya discovered she was Hilal's sister. Immediately after that she'd become so different, so distant; she felt as if she'd lost her. What had happened? Why did Hilal being her brother change everything?

When the cousins left, Dunya asked Suha if she wanted to visit Suad with her.

"She wants to see you."

"Well, I, on the other hand, don't want to see her. As I said, Dunya, no girl can have two mothers. Do you want me to betray the mother who brought me up, who took care of me, who *actually* loved me? I don't think I can do that."

"You don't have to betray her. Anyway, I must go and see Suad."

"No, you must not. You must spend the afternoon with *me*, and you must, I really mean it, you must meet Basma, who is my real mother," Suha smiled cheekily. "You must."

"I must?" Dunya stood up and picked up her bag from the floor. "I must go and visit Suad, and I must find Hilal. And then after that I'll come back and see you and your mother."

Suha grabbed two of Dunya's fingers as she got up. "You're not going anywhere. I've been waiting for you for days and days and days. Do you know how long I waited for you? Let's spend the afternoon together. I want to hear all about you. Last time I told you about myself, now it's your turn to tell me. I thought we were friends, I like you and I thought you liked me. Just because I'm Hilal's sister, doesn't mean you have to suddenly be so formal with me. I liked you the way you were. Let's go back to how we were when we first met, let's continue from there. And don't worry about Hilal—my cousins will bring him to you in a bag of flour or inside a large gateau if that is what it takes. They know lots of dodgy people, don't underestimate them."

"You really think they can get me Hilal back?"

"Yes," Suha said. "I'll make sure they do. He's my brother, isn't he? And perhaps one day I'll love him as much as you do."

"I am sure you'll love him very much. And he'll love you."

"You think so?" Suha sat down. "Look, if Hilal is really my brother, does that not mean you're my sister? Not a bio-logical sister but a sister of the heart. That's even better. If he loves you, I love you too. We're twins aren't we, and don't they say twins have the same heart and the same soul? So if you love him, you must love me! Don't you?" Suha kissed Dunya on the cheek.

"I do," Dunya said, rather shyly.

"Okay then, let me make you my speciality cup of tea to celebrate. Last time you only tried my famous lemonade."

Suha stood by a little gas stove and picked out a little paper bag of sweet-smelling tea leaves and threw them into a teapot with boiling water. She found some sugar, and glasses, set the teapot down and lay on a carpet a little way from Dunya and looked at her. She looked at her the way she had always done, from the beginning, in a way that made Dunya feel overwhelmed with shyness. No one had ever looked at her in that way before, not even Hilal. Dunya distinctly felt the effect that look had on her. How it touched her, how it moved her.

"You're too timid," Suha said to her. "I really don't know if you are the same girl I met in Café Taba. What happened to you?"

"Something did happen."

"I know it's Hilal, I understand," Suha leaned her head sideways and looked at Dunya even more closely. Then she pulled Dunya gently toward her by one of her hands, and rested her head on her shoulder while they both sat down. Their arms were around each other's waists now. The silence between them was loud—louder than a roaring crowd.

Suha moved nearer toward Dunya and lay down on the floor next to her. Their bodies were now brushed one against the other. Dunya's eyes were shut at first, and then she summoned up the courage to half open them, and there she saw Suha. "I want to take a photograph of you," Dunya said to Suha. "Sit on that chair here, beside this cupboard. Close your eyes."

But Suha didn't do as she was told and kept her eyes wide open. How could she ever capture Suha in a single photograph? And how could she be so sure that what she saw inside her viewfinder was not simply a trick of the light? Dunya took a few steps back and focused her lens. She could see Suha, all of her, encompassed in the small rectangle of her lens. She could catch an image of her, something she could keep forever. But when she looked at this photograph in years to come, would Suha have turned into a stranger? Only a few days ago she was a stranger, and in the future she might turn into something vastly unknown again. But at this moment and with this small distance between them, the distancing effect of the lens made Dunya feel less fearful. Dunya didn't know how near or far she wanted Suha to be. A strand of hair half covered one of Suha's eyes and Suha looked at her in such a tender way that she felt her heart melting. This was the moment in time that she wanted to hold forever still. She pressed the shutter button.

"Is that it?" Suha said, getting ready to stand up again.

"No, let me take another one."

Suha looked into Dunya's camera.

Dunya knew that if she looked into Suha's eyes without the camera between them, Suha would easily be able to guess her feelings. Suha looked at Dunya as Dunya was looking at her, while the camera stood between them like a screen behind which each of them could hide. She pulled out a little instrument from her bag and held it near to Suha's shoulder and clicked it.

"What is this?" Suha asked her.

"A light meter to measure the light," Dunya said.

She saw that Suha, like her brother, was a person made up of layers, layers of light and layers of dark. There was light under the dark, and dark under the light. It was something that had so intrigued her in Hilal before, but in Suha it mesmerized her and held her captive. She was like a question in motion.

"Is that it?" Suha said, getting ready to stand up again. "I didn't hear the shutter click. I didn't see the flash. What kind of camera do you use? A silent one?"

Dunya put her camera down on a table nearby. "I can't take this photograph of you any more."

"But you have been taking photographs, Dunya."

"No, I only took one, and I'm not even sure it's going to come out. There's too much light in the room. We must try another day."

"Too much light? What are you talking about? If anything, it is too dark," Suha said. "You are such a strange girl, Dunya, but I can't help but like you. I don't know why."

Suha flirted with Dunya mercilessly that entire afternoon. She'd stare at her, hold her gaze and watch her blush. She'd touch her, lie next to her, and slowly but surely she drove her to feel intense desire for her. Everything the two of them did that afternoon was what new lovers might do, what a boy and a girl falling in love might do, not two girls who are getting to know each other as friends or future sisters-in-law. But she must be careful, Dunya knew, for Suha was surely nothing like Hilal. The most likely possibility was that she was exactly his opposite. Suha could never love her, she had never loved anyone, and if she did it could never be a girl—such a possibility would never occur to her. She was nothing but a habitual seductress who flirted without thinking about it, unconsciously, innocently, without a purpose or intention. Perhaps Dunya's impressionability and all too transparent adoration amused her a little and made her want more of it, a little more every time. Perhaps it flattered her or entertained her. It was nothing but a game to her.

Suha stood in front of the mirror and began to take her dress off. Then she threw it on the floor. She took off her tights and then she washed her face with water and took off all of her makeup. She was still as, if not more, beautiful than ever like this.

She opened the wardrobe and began to rummage inside it. "Here," she shouted, "this is just perfect." She threw a man's light summer suit on a chair.

"What are you doing, Suha?"

Suha pulled out a gray-haired wig and a French beret from one of the drawers. Then she grabbed a box from under the wardrobe and stood in front of the mirror, applying tens of different types of makeup to her face. A little bit of this and a little bit of that, a short, thick mustache here and an eyebrow there, men's cologne and something that looked like extra neck hair.

"You look like a really smug old man."

"I look like a typical, lovely, Christian, middle-aged man from Latakia. Can't you see?" Suha walked around the room proudly.

"Even your walk's so deliberate, stiff-legged and full of belly! Why are you wearing this?" Dunya came near to Suha and touched the cushion she'd added as padding on her belly.

Suha pushed her away.

"You'll make my clothes smell of your perfume and then we'll both be in trouble with my wife, love of my life. She won't be happy."

"How could anyone be interested in you, in more than a platonic sort of way? Tell your wife, love of your life, she has nothing to worry about. You're out of harm's way, looking like you do."

"You're cruel."

"Just honest." Dunya smiled. She paused a little to think, surveyed Suha's new appearance once more and laughed quite loudly. "So what's the plan?"

"I'm planning to take you on a little trip. Do you have some money?"

"Why?"

"Because I don't."

"And?"

"You'll see."

Dunya felt more relaxed now that Suha had turned into a fatherly old man. She walked arm in arm through the city with her and then they found a taxi, which took them out of town. For a couple of hours it drove them south of the city while they continued to hold hands. Finally, when they

185

were somewhere that looked like *nowhere*, a large, walled compound became visible in the distance: Aleppo Army Headquarters.

"Thank you, driver, just drop us here please and come back for us in an hour," Suha told the driver with a pitch-perfect impression of a well-heeled patriarch from Latakia. "Daughter, pay the driver," she said to Dunya. "Women. They hold all the purse strings nowadays."

The driver looked as if he agreed. With a tone of bitter tragedy in his voice, he added, "It's a sign the world is going to end."

The Aleppo barracks looked rather terrifying. The wall around it was made of breezeblock upon unpainted breezeblock rising about ten meters high. Above the last row, a sharp line of colored broken glass followed the building round like a noose.

All along the walls, and painted with thick brushes dipped in black paint, were repetitions of the following sentence:

Long Live Hafez al-Assad!

"Stop! Put your hands up in the air!"

Dunya and Suha raised their hands up in the air and looked ahead of them at a soldier with a ruthless-looking face (punctuated by a pair of big, soft, long-lashed eyes).

"We weren't planning on playing in a cowboy movie," Suha said rather impatiently.

"Who are you two? What are you doing here? And who has given you permission?" the soldier demanded.

"We are here on urgent business," Suha said, puffing up her chest in a gesture of proud defiance and putting her hands in her pockets. "We don't have time to get permission. It's a matter of life and death, young mister. We're here to look for a husband for my daughter." Suha pointed at Dunya with her index finger as if to illustrate her point.

The soldier examined Dunya carefully. "Well, that's a rather novel way of going about it, Sir. Yes, your daughter is very pretty. And yes, our camp is packed with men, most of whom are single. But we're not here to get married. We're here to save our country."

"I'm only looking for one particular future husband, young man, and I hear he might be one of you."

"I'm sure many men here would find your daughter delightful, but this is neither the time nor the place," the soldier said.

"Well, sir, it's not as simple as you might think. It's far more complicated than that. Is there someone by the name of Hilal Shihab in this camp?"

"Why? All such information is confidential."

"He's my poor daughter's fiancé. Their wedding was scheduled for last week and Mr. Hilal Shihab disappeared into the army a day earlier, thus abandoning my daughter and dishonoring her! What he did was unacceptable and no father worth his salt would accept it. Would you?" Suha said to the soldier, trying to incite his chivalrous feelings. "I knew I was risking my life coming here, but what father wouldn't do that for his dear daughter?" Suha put her arms around Dunya's shoulders. "She's brokenhearted." Suha looked at Dunya with pity and despair. "And as you know, heartbreak is a fate worse than death, particularly for women."

"Is it?" The soldier inspected Dunya with great pity.

"Yes, of course," Suha said in a melancholy voice. "And that's why you must help us find that damned Mr. Shihab urgently, and we must be allowed to borrow him from you for a day or two and take him to the mosque and get the sheikh to marry them immediately. We have no time to waste. She's in love with him, and she refuses to marry anyone else. I will not allow her to turn into a spinster, just because Mr. Hilal Shihab decided to join the army at an unsuitable moment."

"But it's a national duty."

"Of course, of course. I couldn't agree with you more. I love my country, too. I worship the president as we all do. But Hilal *must*, he must be found and he must, he must marry her. It's a matter of life and death. You understand? If we wait until he comes out of the army, she'll be too old and he won't want her any more. Do you understand?"

"Yes," said the soldier, in a surprisingly understanding tone, "but there are 2,002 men in this compound and how am I to find that one highly irresponsible young man among them?"

"Don't you have records of him?"

The soldier seemed confused. He was a sweet man at heart, and when he thought a little about it, he realized that he really had no idea why he was standing there with a gun in his hand and pointing it at a doting father and his upsettingly pretty daughter, whose youth could fade at any moment during the next three to four years.

"Okay," he said in a rather mellow tone of voice, as if he'd made up his mind. "I'll go and ask at the office."

"You're an honorable man. I knew it from the moment I saw you," Suha called out loudly as the soldier turned his back and goose-stepped to the barracks.

Dunya and Suha sat on a stone with their backs to each other, waiting for the soldier, looking completely out of context. If anyone who knew them saw them now they would surely have said to them, "Are you completely out of your minds? Run back home, run right away! Run back home, you insane girls!" This was no place for two young women to hang out, especially not in costume.

They sat with their backs to one another on a rock; their shoulder blades touching, their spines parallel.

Behind them was a long asphalt road that looked like a giant snake ready to pounce on someone and destroy their trust in nature forever. In front of them was the barracks. The sound of soldiers marching could be heard like a constant thud or a nervous heartbeat. And every now and then a testosterone-fuelled scream would blare out of the loudspeakers, which looked like diminutive satellite dishes:

Left, right, left, left, right, left, right.
STOOOOP.
Sons of bitches!
Donkeys, morons, oxen and owls!

To their left and to their right, the edge of the Syrian desert began, a desert whose name they didn't know and whose smell they had never smelled, a smell of dust and dry air—a smell of something baking. The air moved in fits and starts, causing shadowy clouds of dust to move around them. They had to close their eyes. Half an hour went by, and then they heard the sound of boot-steps. When they opened their eyes and looked at the ground, they saw a cloud of dust. And just above it, a soldier's boot.

They both stood up. "Have you . . . ?" they asked in one voice.

"No one named Hilal is stationed here," the soldier said in a firm official tone.

"He must be!" Suha said.

"He isn't."

"Where is he then?" Suha asked.

"He's not here. That's all I know. No more."

"But I happen to know that he is."

"Where was he born?" the soldier asked.

"Aleppo," Suha answered. "Don't all Aleppo boys get sent here first? That's what I heard. I'm one hundred percent sure that Hilal is here. He must be here."

"I must go," the soldier said.

"But we need your help."

"I'm of no help to you," the soldier said in very low voice, "find someone more powerful than me to get your message across to Hilal."

"So he is here?" Suha raised her manly voice.

"Sh, sh, sh . . ." The soldier whispered.

Suha inserted a small brown envelope into the pocket of the soldier's army shirt—just above his heart. "Here's a note for him, in case you find him later."

The soldier handed the envelope back to Suha.

"I can't take this. If they find it on me they'll make mincemeat out of me, and then a casserole."

"Tell him Dunya came to see him, promise me you will," Dunya whispered to the soldier.

"I promise," the soldier whispered back. He then turned around and walked away, as if ashamed of himself; his rifle swaying left and right from its holster like a little mast, he marched back into the barracks.

In the background Dunya and Suha could hear the Syrian national anthem playing from the loudspeakers:

Syria my beloved!
You have returned my pride to me.
You have returned my freedom!

Soon the taxi drove up behind Suha and Dunya at great speed, nearly hitting Suha. Were it not that the driver's exceptionally large foot pushed the break violently to the ground, this story might have come to a sudden and tragic end right there.

"You could have killed her!" Dunya told the driver.

"Her?"

"Enough of that now. To the center of town, Mister!" Suha instructed the driver in a gruff voice. She then put her arms around Dunya and kissed her hair to comfort her. Dunya was shaking like a leaf, and could no longer contain her tears.

How could Hilal be inside such a camp? And how were they going to get him out? What if they were hurting him? What if they were beating him?

"You spoil her too much," the taxi driver said.

"Can you just drive please, and focus on the road?" Suha said. "Aren't you far too nosy for a taxi driver?"

"It's our job to be nosy, Sir. We are the eyes and ears of the nation!" (It is a well-known fact that a fair percentage of taxi drivers in Syria moonlight as paid government spies).

Suha leaned over to whisper something in Dunya's ear.

"He's not your father. I'm no fool," the taxi driver said loudly and then he winked knowingly. "You two are in love, aren't you?" he shouted.

When the taxi dropped them in the city center, Suha paid the driver and then ripped her mustache off and stuck it on his face. "Thank you," she said to him in a sensual, feminine, husky-dusky voice. "You should become a detective."

She had a spare mustache in her pocket for the short walk home.

20

In Basma's House

DUNYA COULD HEAR SLOW FOOTSTEPS coming down the staircase, the shuffling of cloth on cloth, cloth on walls, breathlessness. "Where have you been?" a woman's voice came from above. Soon a woman with a bun, large hips, and a bosom hidden under a loose, black dress appeared at the bottom of the staircase. She was clearly a widow, clearly broken, but also clearly full of love for her daughter.

"This is my new friend Dunya," Suha said to her mother.

Basma examined Dunya from top to toe. She could tell just from looking at Dunya and how she dressed and carried herself that she came from another world, where neither she nor her daughter had ever set foot. She was Syrian, but not the way they were.

"Hello, Mrs. Habibi," Dunya said.

"What has Suha been doing to you? Oh, Suha." Basma brushed some flour off the top of Dunya's hair and then ushered them both upstairs to her dining room. "I have a pan of stuffed zucchini with yogurt simmering on the stove." Basma gestured for Dunya to sit next to Suha's usual chair at the table, "Let me feed you."

She laid out a plastic tablecloth on the table, along with three white porcelain plates and forks and spoons and salt and a bowl of green peppers and cucumbers. Then she brought over a bottle of water from the fridge and three cans of Pepsi. "Do you like Bebsi?" she asked (as there is no 'p' in

Arabic), pouring one into a glass for Dunya without waiting for an answer.

Seeing Suha sitting next to Dunya that evening at her dining table made Basma see Suha differently, though she did not know why. Suha seemed so happy, full of delight, and there was something dark and fiery and jewel-like in her eyes that she had never seen before.

"Suha told me you were a singer," Dunya said, munching on some pistachios that Basma had just brought over.

"This isn't supposed to be public knowledge." Basma frowned as she put a napkin stand on the table.

"I don't tell other people, Mama, but Dunya's different and she lives in London. People there don't think songstresses like us are fallen women."

"When did I become a songstress, Suha? We have no songstresses in our family. You're not a songstress," Basma said matter-of-factly.

"Suha was born to be a singer, Mrs. Habibi, I can't imagine her being anything else, she's gifted. She told me it was you who taught her and that you also have a most beautiful voice."

"Did she now? Well, my daughter likes to exaggerate. I have the voice of a crow, if the truth be told. Suha, yes, I can't deny, sings like a bulbul bird. But, and this is what's most important, I hope, Dunya, that you will not be a bad influence on her. She's my only daughter, and I must take good care of her until she finds a husband."

"I want Dunya to hear your voice. . . . Mama, sing to her."

"Oh, Suha." Basma raised her eyebrows but tried to hide her disapproval. It was not polite to be too strict on her daughter in front of such a modern-looking guest, who would not understand it and think of her as backward. Basma was very sensitive to other people's opinion of her and was addicted to being thought of as a good and even *ideal* mother. But people's idea of such a mother varied so vastly and radically from city to city, from town to village, from country to country, and from one era to another. And this girl here, Basma could see, came from a world other than the one she and her daughter inhabited. She would not understand why she had to be so strict with Suha.

"I'd love to hear you sing. Please, Mrs. Habibi, sing," Dunya pleaded.

"If you insist that you want to hear my voice, then I'll sing for you. But please don't tell Suha that she was born to be a singer. That isn't true. She was born to love and be loved by a good man and her children and family. A woman can't have both love and fame, she must choose. Do you want her to be forever lonely, and not to give me beautiful grandchildren?"

Basma reached under the sofa and took her oud out. She sat crossed-legged on her sofa. And when she sang she did not look broken any more—but whole.

Her voice reminded Dunya of the beautiful voices of female singers of the golden age. She was clearly a great talent, and to hide it must have killed her. When a candle hides its light, where does the fire go? Dunya always imagined that if inner fire (just like real physical fire) is not used to create, then what else can it do but destroy? Had Basma destroyed large parts of herself and was she now attempting to do the same to Suha—in the name of love?

After they'd eaten the delicious zucchini in yogurt, Dunya begged Suha to sing too. "Now *you* sing, sing for me."

Suha took out her notebook and her mother's oud. She leafed through a few pages. "I wrote this song for you," she whispered in Dunya's ear. She tested the strings and then began to sing.

Suha's voice was not the same as the hakawati's voice, but so much more. It was a voice impossible to imagine, impossible to resist. It rose and fell like a waterfall, like the waves of the sea or the winds of a galaxy. It filled the room and circled Dunya's heart like a noose, it hypnotized her. Was Suha's song a prayer or a plea? What did she want from her? Dunya looked at Suha and watched and heard the lyrics and the words arising from the root of Suha's heart. Dunya had never seen someone sing like that before, and never for her.

> I am here,
> Because you can see me.
> If you can't see me, I disappear.

She tapped her oud gently. She looked at the floor and then at the ceiling and out of the window and took a deep breath.

> Hold me, or I'll fly.
> Hold me in your arms.
> Hold me in your eyes.
> I am here because you can see me.
> If you can't see me,
> I disappear.

Suha repeated the words of her song, over and over again. And while she did it, she did not look at Dunya, nor at Basma. She only looked at her oud, and occasionally out of the window.

The evening passed and Suha and Basma and Dunya chatted and polished off the zucchini, as well as part of a tray of freshly made kenafeh dessert.

Dunya stood up and looked out of the window of Basma's house where she saw the roofs of hundreds of houses and the tops of alleyways moving across the city in infinite lines and shapes. She listened to the barking of dogs, the meowing of stray cats, and the sound of the last cars reaching their homes in time for the midnight prayer, the call to which boomed high above the city. She had missed her last train back to Latakia.

*

Mrs. Habibi's bathroom was old fashioned. It had a tap and a tiled floor. There was a little gas stove with a metal tub on it.

"We heat the water here," Suha explained. "And then you can add cold water from this tap."

She struck a match and lit the gas.

There was a little wooden seat where one could sit, and a porcelain jug with which to pour water over one's body.

"This is for you." Suha gave Dunya a square piece of soap made of a natural material called ghaar. "And here's a towel." She gave her a large white towel. She held Dunya's wrist for a moment and then let it go.

Suha looked at her, and Dunya looked away. All she wanted to do was kiss her lips, run her fingers through her hair.

Suha turned around and went to her bedroom.

"Wait," Dunya wanted to say to Suha, but she didn't. *Wait, wait, wait.*

Perhaps if this had been a dream, she might have said it out loud: "Wait, wait, wait."

Suha's room was very small and her bed very big. It filled most of the room. She was already under the cover when Dunya came in and sat on a chair nearby. "Where shall I sleep? Don't you have a spare mattress?"

"Come," Suha said. "You can sleep here." She lifted her bedcover.

Dunya lay down quietly next to Suha. She tried to keep a space between them so that no part of her touched Suha's body. Suha switched off the light.

Dunya closed her eyes.

"Why are you so scared?" Suha asked her in the dark, "Are you scared of me?"

"I'm not scared," Dunya said.

"Then why are you so silent and why are you hiding your eyes from me, when you were so open and clear before, when you used to look at me?"

"I'm not hiding anything."

"Then why is your heart beating so fast? I can hear it."

"It isn't beating fast," Dunya said.

Suha took Dunya's hand and laid it on her own heart.

"My heart is beating for you, at least I can be honest. I'm not afraid of how I feel for you. I love you. I never imagined I'd say this to anyone, let alone a girl. How could I have imagined that love would finally come to me like this, in the unexpected form of girl?"

"How do you know it's love? Maybe it's not."

"I love you even though you're a cowardess. And you love me too. I can see it, Dunya. You can't hide it from me."

"Don't say this, Suha, it's not true," Dunya whispered in the dark.

"Why should I not say it?" Suha laid her head on Dunya's chest. "I love you . . . and you love me. It's very simple."

"No, it's not true. Please don't say things like that, Suha, don't say it."

"I don't care if you're a boy or a girl," Suha murmured. "I don't care if it is wrong or right. I love you. *I love you*, the way a boy might love a girl, or a girl might love a boy. Even if you were a bird I'd love you, if you were a stream I'd love you, if you were the dust in the air, even if you were the wind, the breeze I breathe, even if you were a flower, a fragrance, a sound, a song, I'd love you."

Both Dunya's and Suha's hearts were beating so loud now that both of them could hear it. Their heartbeats broke the silence of the room. *Could Basma, who slept in the room beside them, also hear it?* Dunya wondered fearfully. And not only Basma, but everyone who passed in the street outside must also be able to hear their hearts, and the neighbors, and the birds on the trees outside, everyone without exception must be able to hear the sound of her and Suha's guilty hearts.

Dunya gently moved Suha's hand away from her, and her head to the cushion beside her, and then she turned around and lifted the bedcover over her face and hid underneath it. "Let's go to sleep," she said.

Suha lifted the cover too over her head and kissed the back of Dunya's neck. She kissed her on her left shoulder blade, behind her heart, and she circled her arms around her.

"I will love you, even if you don't love me. I don't care. You can love him and I'll love you. If you want to lie to me, lie. I'll still love you. Perhaps your heart is too small for a love as big as this."

Dunya was so quiet now, so still, and she didn't reply.

She must stay quiet, very quiet, she must stay still.

It was dark in the room, very dark, and Dunya could hardly breathe.

Then Suha kissed her and, no, she could not resist her.

Suha kissed her and Dunya kissed Suha, on the lips, on the hair, on her neck, on her cheeks. She kissed her.

Suha's hair was black like the night, her cushion was white, white, white, but all that Dunya could see when she dared to sneak a look at her was *light*. Her body was bathed in light, her limbs, her eyelids, her lips, her hair, she loved everything about Suha, every single part of her.

The only light that came into Suha's bedroom that night sneaked in through the cotton curtain that covered her bedroom window. It only allowed in the diffuse light of street lamps, the reflected light of midnight trucks and cars and motorcycles, and the mysterious light of the moon.

The two of them held on to one another that entire night, as tightly as they could, and it was as if they were flying together inside a small plane without a pilot that was heading very fast toward the stars, but which both of them knew would eventually crash without mercy into the rocky earth.

In their flight they saw things that they had never seen anywhere else: how passion can be terrible and terrifying and how pleasure can be terrible, too, when it is mixed with fear and pain, and the certain knowledge that you can't have what you want to have and that at the very moment you have it, you will also lose it.

"So do you still not love me?" Suha asked Dunya the next morning. "Do you still love him more?"

"Yes," Dunya said. "I love him more."

She looked away from Suha.

"I don't believe you," Suha said.

Dunya took her camera out of its bag, and she didn't say anything to Suha. She looked at her through her lens. She saw Suha's face again that morning with the light of dawn surrounding her own brilliant light. She just wanted to lie down at Suha's feet and admit her love to her.

Suha spread her bare arms out, she sat on her bed and behind her two large palm leaves looked like wings.

What if she had met her first? Would she then be the One and only One?

She clicked her shutter.

Two decades or so ago in the old city of Aleppo, a boy astronomer whose parents hid the truth from him behind a veil of sadness and a girl with a beautiful voice, which she was forced to hide behind a wall of silence, were growing up only a few kilometers apart, each with a hole in their heart, not knowing in what shape or form the truth would come.

Never did it occur to either of them that the truth would come in the shape of a girl whose name was Dunya. And whose fate it was both to bring them together—and to divide them.

21

The Dangers of Love

DUNYA'S RETURN TO LATAKIA WAS, both her parents agreed, a disgrace. "How could you come and go like this? Do you hate us? We're not a hotel, you know," Patricia said. As far as Joseph was concerned, Dunya had achieved the height of irresponsibility and the apex of ingratitude. His fury boiled within and instead of lashing out, he decided that he was going to have to resort to his last weapon: a frozen silence. But the official word-strike only began the next day, six days exactly after Dunya and Hilal's fateful landing in Syria.

Joseph had always had an obsession with the meaning of words. Words and the withholding of words could be used as weapons, he believed. Words and their possible meanings could change history and explain the universe. Words were meaning. There was no meaning without words.

Despite his fascinating insights, Joseph was normally far too busy to explore language fully and had decided early on to confine his researches mainly to patriotic pursuits. His primary objective was to prove that every important word in the world had an Arabic root: Coffee came from 'qahwa,' didn't it? Sugar from 'sukkar,' rice from 'ruz," alcohol from 'al-kuhoul,' and so on. And let us not forget that the Arabs called Portugal 'Burtuqal' (the Arabic word for oranges) because it was full of orange trees.

Joseph sat in his boxer shorts on the sixth floor with a dictionary between his legs, trying to find more evidence of why Arabs were so superior, and didn't notice the girls strolling in the street below. There were girls in rather short skirts strutting their stuff on the main catwalk this side of the Mediterranean: Baghdad Street. Other girls showed off their mascara and eyeliner through carefully chosen headscarves. They sometimes showed some ankle underneath long, suggestive skirts. Men of all shapes and sizes walked around together, hand in hand sometimes, sometimes looking at the girls, sometimes passing them little notes. Sometimes they just tantalized them by ignoring them, smoking and talking about guess what? Politics. Politics was every man's mistress, while every woman's fantasy lover was, of course, who else but Hafez al-Assad?

Joseph hardly noticed any of these boys and none of these girls, as all he was concerned with was finding the roots of more words and blocking off dark thoughts about his daughter's future and the way she seemed to have no respect for him. Patricia was going that way too. He'd tried his best, but he was losing his grip on the women in his life.

Among the girls whom Joseph didn't notice walking up and down Baghdad Street were Dunya and Maria, who were conducting their latest top-secret conversation. They whispered to one another because, particularly during these en masse evening walks, a girl needed to be wary of dedicated eavesdroppers who walked too near and tried to overhear tête-à-tête conversations in order to increase their stocks of freshly harvested gossip.

"One of the top brigadier generals in the northern territories of Syria," Maria whispered, "is extremely keen on Mr. Saddiq's youngest sister. Saddiq told me that he could, if you wanted him to, arrange for Hilal to have a day or two's holiday to come and see you. After that he'll work on trying to get him out altogether, but it will happen step by step, and it will depend on who's pulling the strings on the other side, and if they have more clout than my darling Saddiq."

Dunya stood in the middle of Baghdad Street and put her arms around Maria. "Are you sure of this?" she said.

"Of course, darling," Maria said. "I have no doubt that Saddiq's sister is more than capable of tipping the balance of power in our favor, I promise you, Dunya!"

"Is there anyone in this country who doesn't have their eyes on someone and who's not plotting a marriage? I thought this was a dictatorship, not an enormous dating bureau!" Dunya said as they walked back home.

"There's not much difference between love and a dictatorship, is there?" Maria said. "It's practically the same thing."

"Maybe," Dunya said, "what we've read about in books of poems and heard about in songs was not true after all? Maybe we were wrong," Dunya said to Maria. "I am not sure any more whether I believe in love, you know, the sort of love we always used to talk about and dream of. Believing in it can bring you ruin, it's like falling into the arms of a tiger."

"Are you telling me Hilal is like a tiger? Well, I can't wait to meet him. He sounds like a very intriguing young man." Maria raised her eyelashes until the mascara touched the base of her eyebrows, leaving a line of little black dots.

It was the first time in her life that love had turned into a tiger in Dunya's eyes. Falling in love with Suha was like falling into the arms of a tiger. In its grip, what could she do? If she ran, it would chase her; if she fought it, it would catch her. She silently cried out to Hilal in her mind, *How can I love her like that when I love you? She is not you!*

That evening Joseph went to the lounge and sat in the chair he always chose to sit in when he was at the end of his tether. He turned the TV on to crowd out the terrible thoughts that were whirling through his head.

"Don't you want to eat something, Joseph?" Patricia asked him.

Joseph said nothing and focused his eyes on the TV screen where an eighteen-year-old female soldier was decapitating a snake.

"This is what we're going to do to our enemies," she announced in a sexy but rather scary voice, just before the TV screen relapsed into an orgy of flags and horse hooves accompanied by camp, hero-worship music.

A few days later the doorbell rang at Dr. Noor's residence. When Amina the housekeeper opened the door, she found a young woman wearing a tight, bosom-hugging, red dress and behind her stood two tall men dressed in what seemed to her rather dapper suits. They stood so tall that she had to raise her head to see their faces.

"Is this the residence of Miss Dunya Noor?" the young woman asked. "We need to speak to her urgently."

"Dunya's not in." Joseph arrived in a cloud of aftershave and uttered his first sentence for days.

"When will she be back?" Suha asked him.

"Who knows?" Dr. Noor looked at Suha's red dress with puzzlement. Who was this girl? To him she looked like some 1970s movie actress who had escaped from the silver screen, while the two men who stood beside her looked like vagabond gangsters who reeked of cheap cologne. He hadn't seen girls like this in Latakia, nor men like that. They certainly didn't look like they belonged to the right sort of families.

"How do you know my daughter?" Dr. Noor looked at Aziz and Badri and examined their ill-fitting suits and their trousers and jackets that were far too short, and then, without really meaning to, he burst into a big belly laugh.

The cousins looked at Dr. Noor's well-bred appearance, at the marble floors inside his apartment, the crystal chandelier above his head, and his servant Amina standing obediently a few meters behind him, and they felt small.

"What are you laughing at, Dr. Noor?" asked Suha.

"Nothing. If you tell me who you are, I'll tell Dunya you came by."

"I *am* here, Dad." Dunya came up behind him with a glass of water in her hand. "Suha?" she gasped. She looked at Suha and Suha looked at her, in a way that Joseph *noticed*.

"What's the matter with you two?" Joseph shook his daughter's shoulders as if to wake her up from a reverie. "Look at you and look at her! How do you two know each other? Who is this girl? Tell me, Dunya. On what street corner did you find her?"

"She's Suha from Aleppo. Come in, Suha," Dunya said. "Come in, Aziz, come in, Badri."

Joseph had had it up to *here*. What was it with his daughter and her riffraff friends? He took a second look at Suha as she walked in through his door and for a moment he understood what Dunya must have seen in her. She was beautiful. She was not the sort of ordinary pretty girl that one might find any-where; she had something much more marvellous than that. Even when Joseph, in his angry mood, looked at her, he could almost hear a song, although he could have sworn that the hallway was silent and that there was no song. How unusual for such a common girl to be so uncommonly striking, Joseph thought to himself. And when Suha and Dunya sat across from each other on opposite armchairs, Joseph could not help but observe and secretly admire the quality Suha possessed which reminded him of his own daughter; it was clear that she was the sort of girl who did not follow any rules except those of the heart—a very dangerous sort of girl.

Dunya looked at Suha with both desire and fear. She wished she could be as reckless as her. Look at her, look at her. Why had she not met her first, and then Hilal?

Every time Suha looked at her, Dunya knew that she could see the truth in her eyes, of how much she loved her.

Dunya focused her eyes on Joseph who was sipping from a cup of tea and begrudgingly biting into a biscuit. Patricia arrived and shook everyone's hand and looked a little startled. *Who are these people?* she asked herself. She looked at Dunya with a slightly raised eyebrow.

"And so, Miss Suha, what do you do? Are you a wife, a mother, or a member of the working classes like me?" Joseph poured himself some water.

"I'm a baker," Suha answered blithely.

Joseph gulped.

"You don't look like one," he said.

"Well, you don't look like a doctor," Suha replied.

"Don't I?" Joseph gave her a sharp look. "Dunya, I didn't realize you were now mixing in the sophisticated circles of bakers? I thought Hilal came from tailoring stock."

"He does," Dunya said.

"We are his cousins," Suha said.

"Fine lineage," Joseph smiled.

"Well, you look like you could be a baker yourself, Sir," Suha said after pretending to study Joseph's face closely.

"What do you mean?"

"I'm not sure. You just look like some bakers I know. They're delightful people." She put one of her hands on her hips.

"Really?" Joseph wasn't sure whether to take this as an insult or a compliment—*a baker?*

"Do you not like Hilal because he's poor?" Suha asked him.

"Is he poor?" Joseph said. "I had no idea." He drank more water. "As I said to Dunya before, I would help him if he'd been my son-in-law. But he's not. I'm a very busy man."

"You would have helped him if he'd been a banker from good Greek Orthodox stock, wouldn't you?" Dunya said.

"Don't forget that bakers *make* bread. Bankers make money in order to buy their bread." Suha took a loud slurp from her glass of water.

Joseph bit his tongue. Who was this Suha character anyway? And did her parents not teach her that it was rude to upstage a man in his own home?

"Is she really a baker?" Patricia whispered in Dunya's ear.

"Yes."

"And why is she here?"

"She's trying to help me find Hilal."

"A baker will help you?" Patricia grinned. "You've been away from this country for too long, darling."

Suha waited a little longer before she said anything.

"It's difficult to know whether to hide the truth, or tell it as it is," she said. "What do you think, Dunya? Shall I tell the truth, or shall I hide it?"

"What truth?" Dunya said.

"The truth about what happened to Hilal and why he's in the army and who put him there and who can get him out?"

"Of course you should tell it," Dunya said.

"You want to know even if what I have to say might be painful to hear, or might cause you a psychological and moral shock? Do you think you can handle the truth?" Suha looked at Joseph.

"Yes," Dunya said.

"How about you, Dr. Noor, can you handle the truth?"

"What has it got to do with me?" Joseph said impatiently.

"It has everything to do with you, Dr. Noor," Suha said. "Do you want me to tell your wife and daughter the truth, or shall I hide it from them? It's your choice."

"What are you talking about, Miss Suha? What are you trying to imply? Do I detect a tone of blackmail in your voice?"

"If you help us release Hilal from the 'army' and if you bring him home to his mother *today*, safe and sound, I'll keep my mouth firmly shut," Suha said. "If that is blackmail, so be it."

Patricia looked at Joseph with anxious eyes and held his hands.

"No one talks to me like this!" Dr. Noor stood up. "Who do you think you are? Speak the truth, tell lies, I don't care. No one in their right mind would believe a frivolous girl like you in a silly red dress. What a joke. Who exactly are you to come here to my house and tell me what's what?"

"Very well then," Suha said. "It was your father who . . . who did it," Suha said to Dunya.

"My father who did what?"

"He paid a corrupt army officer to 'recruit' Hilal into the world-famous Elite Brigade induction program, for a total of four years with no holidays."

"Nonsense!" Joseph said at the top of his voice. "Don't believe a word she says. Complete and utter *nonsense*."

"Well, according to the coffee boy and the cleaning lady at the Aleppo barracks," Aziz said in a deep but calm voice, "a man called Dr. Joseph Noor paid the lieutenant to keep Hilal under lock and key, and his best friend Salman Ghazi brokered the deal. Is your name not Joseph Noor and is your best friend's name not Salman Ghazi?"

"How dare you speak to me like this? I am *Dr.* Noor! Who are you? You're nothing but a shoeshine boy, a street sweeper, a sewer rat!"

"The lieutenant at the Aleppo barracks," added Aziz, "runs the barracks as a sort of alternative hotel service. This is how he moonlights to generate a lucrative secondary stream of income, to top up his meager army salary. You all know the economic situation, don't you? A man's gotta do what a man's gotta do," he winked. "Not everyone can be a successful doctor like you, Dr. Noor."

"What an entrepreneur, eh?" Suha said, looking at Dr. Noor.

Joseph looked at Patricia, who had pulled her shaking hand away from his ice-cold hands.

"We need to speak to you in private, Miss Dunya. Do you have a moment?" Badri asked.

"You're not welcome here," Joseph said. "I've had it up to here with Hilal and his ragtag army of down-and-outs!" He shooed Suha and her cousins away with his hands. "Get out!"

"Dad? Is it true what Suha said?"

"What reason do I have to lie?" Suha asked.

"I told you, *she's lying.*" Joseph looked at Suha angrily. "Who is this girl anyway? Why do you believe her over your own father?"

Suha took a piece of paper out of the large envelope she was holding and gave it to Dunya and Patricia, who both read it with their mouths agape:

Receipt

Attention: Dr. J. Noor (Latakia District)

This is to confirm delivery of item and payment for the delivered item and to confirm that instructions regarding the item will be fulfilled for the duration of four years, no more, unless additional, more generous funds are made available.

Yours Truly,

Lieutenant Qasem Bakr al-Shughour

(It was a fateful and fortunate accident that Lieutenant Qasem Bakr al-Shughour's personal tea maker and tea glass washer and server, Bilal, was Badri's brother-in-law, and he was able to copy this receipt and find out all the rest with great ease and some highly risky and courageous eavesdropping.)

"Joseph. Tell me you didn't do it, Joseph." Patricia looked like she was about to explode. "Joseph?"

"Corrupt! You are corrupt!" Dunya said. "Your are selfish and corrupt! Is that why you have friends in the Baath Party, and in the army? Because you're selfish, ruthless, and corrupt like them? Because you're one of them? Hilal's only crime was that he was in love with me, and I with him! For this you're prepared to destroy his life, his career, and his future before it even began? Since when did love become a punishable crime?"

Instead of looking at his wife or his daughter, Joseph looked out of the window for a minute and enjoyed the view of the Mediterranean. The weather was rather windy today, he noticed. Yes, perhaps there would be rain that afternoon. How unusual for a summer's day. But it would be good for the trees and for the flowers. He began to whistle a tune. And without quite understanding why, the tune that he accidentally began to whistle was the Syrian National Anthem, "Syria my beloved, you have returned my pride to me, you have returned my freedom." How could a daughter and a wife whom he loved so dearly and worked so hard to provide for and protect be so ungrateful to him? He could not understand it. What heart-breaking creatures women were, they were born to break men's hearts, whether as wives or as daughters. How unpredictable they were, what misery they caused. What disgrace and what distress. He really should've never married an English woman, never; his mother was right.

"You are heartless, Joseph, heartless. I married a man without a heart," Patricia said.

"So now it's me who is heartless and lacking in love, not you and your daughter who, instead of worrying about me and my health and happiness, spend all your time worrying about a complete stranger?" Joseph looked deeply hurt. "I was trying to be the head of this house but you two would much rather I was a mouse."

He looked at everyone standing in front of him rather grandly, as if the people who looked at him with such disappointed eyes were no bigger than flies, no more important than cockroaches. With both his hands firmly ensconced in his pockets, he walked out of the room and then out of the house.

"What happened to the Joseph Noor I fell in love with? What happened to the romantic young man for whom I gave up everything?" Patricia said.

*

Later on, Aziz wrote his phone number on the back of a box of matches and gave it to Dunya. "When you have everything ready and you need us, just ring us and we'll turn up, in a flash," he said.

Before leaving, Suha put her arms around Dunya and kissed her behind her ears. Dunya didn't say a word. Soon after that Suha and her two cousins ended their lightning visit to Latakia, and returned to Aleppo in a puff of flour.

Lieutenant Qasem Bakr al-Shughour, who had 'welcomed' Hilal into the army barracks twelve days or so ago, had done so by first confiscating his telescope and then by inspecting his notebook, where he read the following page, which he didn't understand:

A NEW THEORY OF MOONLIGHT
Moonlight is a finger pointing to the sky, asking: why?

I will call the Darkness X and Moonlight Y

$$X + Y = I$$

Who am I?
Who am I?
Who am I?

(Everything looks either black or white in Moonlight).

If it weren't for Darkness there would be no Light.

The Moon only looks so beautiful because of the Night.

"What nonsense," the lieutenant thought to himself. "This man isn't a scientist: he's a girl. Pathetic." He then tore Hilal's notebook up and threw it into the nearest trash can.

"Next time you interrogate him, ask him *why* he looks into the sky so often? Ask him and report back to me," the lieutenant commanded one of his officers whose name was Iyad.

"He's already told me, Sir. He said he's looking for his father."

"Nonsense. If you believe *that*, you'll believe anything." The lieutenant spat on the floor. "Don't relent until he tells you the truth."

After that, the barracks barber shaved all of Hilal's hair off and then swiftly swept it with a broom into a dustpan and threw it out of the window.

Hilal's long black curls were collected by the wind and scattered into the four corners of the Syrian desert.

Early one morning at the Aleppo military barracks, Hilal was hosed down like all the other soldiers, and after grueling morning exercises, a mind-expanding 'Imperialism Post-Hitler' class began.

"We will cure our country from the cancer of Zionism and imperialism," the morose major who was teaching the class growled. "And the only way is with *this*," he threatened, taking his gun out of his back pocket.

"If you don't listen carefully to me I might start practicing on you!" he laughed.

The class full of bald men (who all wished they were tucked up in bed) nodded.

"Hilal Shihab! Stand up! Wake up or I shall push that knife into your head, or empty a bullet belt in you brain, if you'd rather that. Wake up, you foreign girl. This isn't a daydreaming workshop!"

"Yes, Sir."

"I've heard that you've been a bastard recently. You abandoned your bride mid-wedding, didn't you?"

"Did I, Sir?"

"Don't play the innocent! We heard that a decent and law-abiding father is furious with you because you expressly promised to marry his daughter and then joined the army before you fulfilled your promise. Her reputation is now in tatters because of you and she's in danger of becoming a spinster. What sort of man are you? Have you no morals and no decency? We are still amassing evidence about your spying activities, but meanwhile you need to marry the girl in question, whose name is Dunya Noor. This is her father's wish."

"*Her father* wants me to marry her? Are you sure of that? Of course I'll marry her." Hilal was flushed with excitement. Dunya had found him, and not only that but she had also convinced her father that he was the One. What a victory.

"Blushing like a maiden, now? You are, as I've said many times before, pathetic. If you don't tie the knot with her today before sunset you'll be finished, do you hear me? And if you don't come back here by midmorning tomorrow, I'll set my dogs on you. Now get out!"

Mr. Saddiq, big-bellied and big-hearted, was waiting in the Aleppo barracks main reception area with a cigarette hanging out of his mouth. He looked at Hilal with a paternal air. "Are you Hilal?" he asked.

"Yes, and who are you, Sir?"

"This is for you."

In full view of everyone in reception, Mr. Saddiq handed Hilal a transparent bag with a pitch-black bridegroom's suit in it, folded on top of a crisp white shirt. "Go and put it on," he said to Hilal and also handed him a bottle of cologne. "That too."

Behind a rock, behind a tree, behind a stretch of the sea, near the mountain village of Kasab—a popular mountain resort close to Turkey, where Joseph happened to own a holiday home—a white van was parked.

Hilal looked up to the sky at first. The light blinded him and he couldn't see the van for a moment. He had a dark tuxedo on, shiny shoes, and no hair. He walked with his hands covering his eyes. And then gradually he was able to see her: Dunya.

"Dunya." Hilal ran toward her, and she walked faster and faster toward him. But as soon as she was within his grasp and he tried to put his arms around her, she took a step back. She looked at him as if she wasn't sure who he was—or as if she wasn't sure it was him. Yes, she'd never seen him wearing a tuxedo before or without his long unkempt curls, but here he was, *it was him.*

She touched his cheek. "Where were you?" she asked.

"I was busy looking for this." Hilal took a little red flower from his pocket. "And then I lost my way." He noticed how strangely Dunya looked at him. "You shouldn't have worried. I was planning to come back. See?" He pointed at his suit. "I just had to find something suitable to wear to our wedding, and that took time."

"Our wedding?" Dunya said. "What wedding, Hilal?"

"I thought your dad wanted us to get married today?"

"My dad? No, my dad paid the army to kidnap you, he wants to get rid of you and wants me to marry Maria's brother George. Look, Hilal." Dunya pointed behind her to the white van, which was near enough now that he could read the sign inscribed on it: Aleppo Central Bakery. "These men are smuggling us out of the country." She took his hand in hers. "We must hurry." She pulled him behind her.

"Stop," Hilal said. "First, I must kiss you. Kiss me." He took her face into his palms and tried to kiss her, but Dunya moved her lips away from him. He put his arms around her and held on to her waist tightly as if a strong wind was blowing. Why did she not want to kiss him or be held by him? Hilal looked behind Dunya and glimpsed a blonde woman in a pair of flimsy high heels coming out of the van, and soon afterward two mustachioed young men appeared.

"What's your mother doing here?" he asked Dunya. "And who are these men?"

Patricia sat excited as a schoolgirl, next to Aziz, who was sitting between her and Badri, who was driving the van at great speed. He stuck a tape into a cassette player and some extremely melancholy Arab pop music came out.

The Aleppo Central Bakery van slowed down as the border station came into view.

"Please don't say anything, Mrs. Noor," Aziz said to Patricia. "Just look out of the window."

"What do you mean?" she asked him.

"If they ask you what we're carrying in the van, just say bread."

"But what about Dunya and Hilal?"

"Precisely," Aziz said. "Don't mention them. Say we have bread. Or pretend you don't speak Arabic."

The van was now crawling as slowly as a tortoise behind yellow taxis, falling-apart cars, buses, trucks, and motorbikes.

A large brown donkey passed by the van on Patricia's side. It stopped as its head was filling the window frame and looked at Patricia demurely. Patricia rolled the window up in panic.

"Don't worry," Badri said. "He wouldn't dare touch you."

"Wouldn't he?" Patricia said.

"Yasine," Badri called out of his window. "Yasine."

A border guard with a delicate mustache and double stars on his epaulettes recognized Badri and his van. He waved and then walked briskly toward them.

"You're back again, my friends?"

"Yes, we're taking another bread cargo to Istanbul. They only like our bread apparently. They sell it at high prices," he bluffed.

"Mmm, I like it too."

"I know," Badri said, handing the man a large sack filled to the brim with bread.

"Are these top-notch?" Officer Yasine asked.

"Of course they are, my friend," Badri insisted. "And I found these for you too." Badri gave the man three packets of Marlboro cigarettes, and then they shook hands.

In the back of the van Hilal and Dunya sat on a small rug hidden from view by hundreds of loaves of Arabic bread and dozens of large bags of flour.

"Your mother is on her way to Istanbul in a private taxi," Dunya said to Hilal, "and in the taxi with her she has brought you a beautiful white suit which she made especially for you. But also in that taxi is your sister who wants to meet you," Dunya said.

Hilal sat upright. "I don't have a sister. Who is this person who wants to meet me?"

"You have a sister. I accidentally found her," Dunya said, "when I went to Aleppo looking for you." Dunya put her arms around Hilal and hid her face from him by leaning it against his neck. She could feel how hard his heart was beating and how wildly he was breathing. What part of the story could she tell him, and what part must she hide? She was not a skilful liar and Hilal normally read her like a book.

"Her name is Suha," Dunya said now sitting back and trying to look at Hilal directly and appear relaxed. "You won't believe how I found her. She was dressed as a young man who looked just like you. Basically, I thought she was you and so I followed her around the streets of Aleppo."

"Are you making this up? Have you been drinking? My 'sister' looks like a man, a man just like me?"

"She was in disguise you see, theatrical disguise," Dunya said.

"Stop pulling my leg, Dunya." Hilal now laughed. "You are something else. Even on a day like this!" He smiled. "This is why I love you."

"This is no laughing matter Hilal . . . I followed her thinking she was you, then she went into a men's café where she sat on a table and sang a song. She also played the oud. Then I knew she wasn't you since you can't sing, nor can you play the oud. But I thought perhaps she was one of your relations or might know you and I wanted to ask her—him, I mean."

"What fantastical nonsense!"

Hilal's laugh was loud and rang throughout the van.

"Don't laugh, Hilal," Dunya said. "I am telling you the truth."

"So when finally you discovered he was a she, what evidence did she give you to prove that she is my sister? She sounds like a charlatan. She is playing a trick on you and you are so gullible. Oh, Dunya." Hilal took Dunya's hand in his and pulled her nearer to him while the van swayed and swivelled left and right and up and down, and the bags of flour and bread shook and shifted.

"Let me continue," Dunya said. "It is your mother who swears she is your sister. And not only that, but your *twin*."

"My mother says that?" Hilal muttered. "Well, then, she must've lost her marbles. Losing my father and then me disappearing like that, it was too much for her. I have to talk to her. But a sister, no. If I had a sister she would've told me long ago. Why would she hide it?"

"Your mother has confessed to everything, and she will confess it to you once we arrive in Istanbul, and you will then see Suha and you won't have a doubt about her identity. She's basically you, had you been a girl. I swear it."

The Aleppo Bakery van rushed toward the city of Istanbul like some swift, imagined wind. Dunya told Hilal all the parts of the story of her encounter with Suha that she felt she could tell him. Hilal found it very hard to believe any of it, but Dunya continued and then she told him in detail everything that Suad had told her and Suha about how and why she and his father decided to give her up.

As he listened, Hilal lay down on the floor of the van and put his head in Dunya's lap. "All those questions I had, that empty feeling, their dark and endless sadness, their secrecy. I was not imagining any of it? I was being lied to all these years."

This was why he had felt as he had for so long: as if a piece of him had been torn out, as if a piece of him had gone missing. That it was Dunya who had first seen that lost piece in him and who then found it, only made him love her more.

"Kiss me, Dunya," he said.

And Dunya kissed him.

The two of them sat behind columns and columns of bread, which hid them from prying eyes. Some light was streaming in from cracks in the ceiling of the van, which was hurtling along, speeding over Turkish steppes, moving smoothly over Anatolian tarmac, with the two of them stuck in its belly, tears streaming from their eyes. Were they tears of joy or tears of fear—what sort of tears were these?

When Hilal saw his twin sister Suha for the first time since the hour they were born, she was sitting opposite his mother on a table on the balcony of the Ibrahim Pasha Hotel in Istanbul.

He, Dunya, Patricia, and Suha's baker cousins walked toward their table looking like a group of vagabonds after their twenty-four-hour drive from the Syrian border.

Suad cried out when she saw her son. Hilal buried his face in his mother's hair and held her tightly to his chest, even though he was angry with her and wanted to ask her a thousand questions. He let Suad brush off all the flour from his black tuxedo, which smelled of bread and tears. He then dared to look at Suha. "Is she really my sister?" he asked Suad.

"She is," Suad said.

Hilal noticed that as soon as he looked at Suha she turned her eyes away from him and instead looked at Dunya.

"Dunya," she called out. She stood up and put her arms around her. It was as if they had known each other forever. Dunya put her arms around Suha.

Suad pulled Suha up by her hands and brought her near to Hilal. "This is your brother. How could we have done this to you? I don't know how we had the heart to do it. . . ."

"Why are you asking me?" Suha said impatiently. "How am I supposed to know?"

"I understand how you feel," Suad joined Suha's hands to Hilal's and held them both between her palms. "But your brother is another matter. He did not do anything to you. You and he should never have been torn apart and now you must reunite, in the heart. I can see how he loves you even though he does not know it yet or know you. Will you love him too?"

Both Hilal and Suha could see the sorrow and regret that were etched on every line of their mother's face. And she in turn saw the pain in their eyes, the pain whose clumsy author she and their father had been.

Dunya felt deeply ashamed of herself as she looked at Suad holding both her children in her arms, and when she saw how reluctant Suha was to accept her mother's and Hilal's love, and how she looked at her, only at her.

Something about Suha made Hilal want to both run to her and run away. He was no longer a young man alone. It was no longer just him and the moon. There was this other part of him standing there with a mind of her own, and one not very interested in him. Instead of looking at him, she looked at Dunya.

Looking at Suha made Hilal feel that he was looking into a supernatural mirror, where he could see in one instant everything that he was and everything he wasn't.

She went toward Dunya again, opened her arms and put them around her.

"Dunya," he heard her say. She said it in such a tender way.

Dunya held Suha for a moment and kissed her on her cheek. Then she pulled away, "Mum, I want you to meet Hilal's mother." Patricia and Suad stood opposite each other, one on high glittering heels with blond hair and the other one wearing all black, as if she were enveloped in a dark cloud. They were like night and day, but they liked each other anyway.

"Come and help me settle into my room," Patricia said to Suad, "and I will order us something to drink and we can talk more. Let's leave the children to it. I can't make head nor tail of what Dunya has told me. I want to hear everything from you directly." Patricia took Suad's hand in hers and Suha's cousins carried her luggage and trailed behind.

"I don't know you, you don't know me," Suha said to Hilal in an off-hand manner. "Just because we both have black hair, doesn't prove that I am your sister. It doesn't mean a thing. And your mother might've lost her mind, has that occurred to you? There's no evidence of any of the outlandish things she is claiming. I mean, what family gives up their children because of what a coffee cup says?" Suha raised her eyebrows. "Huh?"

"I already have a mother," she went on, "as I already mentioned to your mother. But it is nice to meet you anyway. I've heard a lot about you from Dunya," she said. "And I'm glad you are a free man now and not a soldier. The army does not suit you. Your eyes are made to look at the moon, not through the eyepiece of a rifle. We do have the same eyes, I can see where all the confusion's coming from."

Hilal wanted at that moment to put his arms around his sister, but he resisted the impulse. Despite her more friendly words, frost, invisible frost, seemed to envelop her, separating him from her.

Outside the sun was setting over another day. But this day was unlike any other. "If you had not been lost, I would not have found Suha," Dunya said when she came back, behind her a waiter with a tray of drinks. "You two are like the moon and its dark side: when one of you disappears, the other one appears. But today is unlike any other day, the two have become one. You two should never have been separated." Dunya looked at Hilal and Suha. "I love you both so much." Tears rolled down her eyes and she held Suha with one hand and Hilal with the other.

"You already love her as much as me, even though there is still no evidence she is my sister?" Hilal said. "You do have a lot of charm, Suha, I can vouch for that."

"Today is a strange day," Suha said. "The sort of day I find it hard to believe I am having."

"Why did you come all the way here with Suad if you don't believe that I am your brother or that she is your mother?" Hilal asked.

"I wanted to see Dunya. I thought that if I don't see her today, she might go back with you to London and then I would never set eyes on her again."

"I see," Hilal said. "You two have really hit it off then, haven't you? Maybe you are my sister. Dunya seems to like you as much as me, but I don't like to share her," Hilal said, and he looked at Dunya. He could swear that he saw her blush then.

Dunya linked Hilal and Suha's hands together. "Maybe I can go away with my mother today and you can spend a day together. If you spend some time you will see that you two are twins. You won't be asking for proof. You are two sides of the same coin."

"I am not a coin," Suha said. "Nor half of a single coin. Don't talk like that Dunya, don't say such things. Don't go, stay with us."

"I will go, but I'll come back soon," she said and walked off.

Hilal and Suha continued to hold one another's hands shyly, reluctantly.

Hilal saw that Suha possessed his eyes; he possessed her eyes. It was not just the hair, not just her chin, not just everything about her that reminded him of himself, it was something that went much deeper. If he had met her by accident, somewhere else, in some other time or place, and even if no one had told him who she was, and what she was to him—he would have known. Who else could this beautiful girl be?

He smiled at Suha and took her hand in his again, lifting it toward him. He touched each of her fingers as if counting them one by one and he inspected them. "We have the same fingers," he said. "But yours are so much more delicate. And your lips, they're the same as mine, a more perfect interpretation, and your eyes and your chin, they're all the same as mine, but so exquisite."

"You think so?" Suha took her hand away from Hilal and put it on her lap. "You are how I imagined you to be, how Dunya described you. I'll need time to believe that you're my brother. I will need more time."

She looked away from him.

"Suha," Hilal whispered.

He felt an overwhelming, irrational rush of love suddenly filling his heart. He did not know how this happened, but it did, though he could see that Suha didn't feel the same. He felt shy and confused. How could he not love her, she who was a *part* of him once? The more he looked at her, the more he was convinced that she was the secret of his soul, the fire in his heart. How could she not feel it too? It was hard to understand her indifference. Instead of looking at him, Hilal saw how Suha looked only at Dunya (and when Dunya had gone, at the seat where she had been sitting). Perhaps she would love him one day too; he hoped that she'd love him more than Dunya. He was her brother, wasn't he? Who was Dunya to her?

"Mr. Joseph Noor," the hotel porter announced, walking behind Joseph and carrying his luggage.

Dunya, Hilal, Suha, Suad, Patricia, Badri, and Aziz all looked at Joseph in horror. How had he found them? And what was he going to do now?

Joseph's black curly hair, richly peppered with white streaks, seemed to droop in sorrowful shapes, his soft blue eyes looked at Dunya and Patricia sheepishly. "Good afternoon," he said and sat down on an empty armchair next to Patricia. "A coffee without sugar," he added to the waiter.

After that Joseph did what no one had expected him to do by saying what no one had imagined he would ever say: "*I'm sorry.*"

"I took away from you, Mrs. Shihab, your only son." Joseph addressed Suad first. "I took him away simply because he fell in love with my daughter. I am sorry." He spoke as if he finally understood the gravity of his action. Joseph looked at Dunya in a way that made her feel both happy and afraid: *could this really be happening?* But she couldn't help herself and she ran toward Joseph and put her arms around him.

"I know now where you get your stubbornness from." Tears ran down Joseph's cheeks. "It's from your stubborn father." His words came out with difficulty. He was finding it hard to speak. "How many fathers have a daughter like you?" he said to her, "Someone who never lies, who speaks the truth, who follows her heart, who *disobeys*?" Joseph smiled at Dunya.

Joseph had had an epiphany few people have. It had dawned on him that maybe he was too old-fashioned, too spoiled, too rigidly attached to a bygone past, perhaps it was time that a man like him grew up and tried to learn something from his daughter. Perhaps Dunya and Hilal had the answer, let them try life their way. Living in a dictatorship meant that throughout his life, he, just like the president, could dictate his wishes to anyone who had the misfortune of having less power than him, and he now wondered whether this sort of power could turn any man into a monster.

"Dad," Dunya said in a tearful voice. She felt pity for him, for she could see how crestfallen and confused he was. *If only he knew*, she thought to herself, *if only he knew—that I am no longer the girl I used to be, that I, too, can lie and be untrue.*

Hilal came from behind Dunya and put his arms around her.

"Do you really love her as you say you do?" Joseph asked him.

"Yes," Hilal said, and both Joseph and Dunya and Suha and everyone in the room saw clearly that he meant it. Dunya tried not to look at Suha.

"True love is rare and must not be sniffed at," Joseph looked up at Patricia, who came to his side and kissed him gently on his cheek.

"I'd like to ask first for your forgiveness, Mrs. Shihab, and secondly for your son's hand in marriage for my daughter." Joseph bowed his head and crossed his hands in front of him like a shy schoolboy and waited for Suad's answer. He seemed to be making a supernatural effort to overcome his natural prejudices. Dunya could hardly believe her eyes, or ears. She felt touched to the core, but also unworthy, guilty, confused. She wished she could hide somewhere and never reappear.

"It's for Hilal to decide," Suad said. "As far as I'm concerned, Dunya is made for my son and he for her, as soon as I saw her, I knew."

Hilal lifted Dunya up in his arms with whoops of joy. "It was worth getting kidnapped for this," he laughed. "Wasn't it, Dunya?"

Everyone crowded around the two of them and began to hug and congratulate them, including Aziz and Badri, both of whom lifted Hilal up in the air, and Suad, who covered him with kisses. And as for Suha, well, Dunya saw how Suha ran away. She did not look at Dunya, nor at Hilal, but ran out of the room. She ran and ran through the hotel lobby in her yellow dress and blue summer shoes, and then she disappeared.

"Nobody asked me whether I wanted to be married," Dunya said to Hilal and to her dad. "Yes, I love Hilal, but we are too young to marry, we're too young, aren't we Hilal?"

"Too young? Really?" Hilal looked very sad. "But one day will you marry me? Do you still want to marry me one day?"

"Yes," Dunya uttered that one word faintly and then said no more. After so much rebellion and so much loud proclaiming and all the wild risks she took for him and what she put him through—this one faint word was like a stab in Hilal's heart.

Joseph seemed even more deflated than Hilal, but he did not say anything. *She's never going to change*, he thought to himself. *That poor boy. I bet my full head of hair that he doesn't know what he's letting himself in for.*

Joseph patted Hilal on the back in a gesture of camaraderie.

Later, when Dunya knocked on Suha's hotel bedroom door, Suha did not answer.

Early the next morning when Hilal rushed out of bed to go and find Suha he found his mother standing outside her room. Suad looked at him with her large dark eyes—full of dark pain.

"She's gone," she said.

"Who's gone?" Hilal asked.

Hilal looked at his mother's hands, which were shaking like two leaves on a pale winter tree. In them she held a yellow dress.

"She took everything with her except for this, the dress your father and I made for her." Suad pulled the dress up to her mouth and kissed it, and then she held it to her chest.

"Why does she not want it?" she whispered. "Why does she not want us?"

That day Hilal and Dunya filed a report about Suha's disappearance at the local police station, while Badri and Aziz hired the most expensive private detective in the city of Istanbul to

225

look for her. Every one of them and everyone they knew or met looked for Suha for days and for weeks to come. They looked and they looked; they looked for her everywhere.

But Suha Habibi, unreal daughter of a sad baker, true daughter of people who didn't have the strength to love her, had left nothing behind her: no letters, no words, no sentences, no songs. Not a sign or clue, that could lead anyone to her— not a hint, not a trace.

22

The Last Photograph

IN A WAY, ONE MIGHT say Dunya Noor had always possessed the personality and character suitable for a budding scientist of the future, even though she chose to become a photographer. But her purpose from the beginning was always to discover the Truth about Love and to prove that truth with her camera, which she used exactly as a scientist might use a scientific instrument.

But as with most explorers and scientific pioneers, the very thing that Dunya had believed would lead her to her One True Love and to discovering the Truth about Love, was also the thing that led her to its opposite.

And so to recap. In the beginning, and for a happy period of time, Dunya believed the following:

1. When love occurred, the object of her love would begin to sparkle, because True Love appeared in the unexpected form of light.
2. All she would need to do was to take a photograph of that light if and when it shone in the face of her beloved, and that was how she'd prove that he was the One.
3. For there could only ever be One.

So what was she to do now that her camera had accidentally proven that her theory was so flawed and that she or

227

anyone else might easily find the Light of Love in the faces of not only One person but Two?

(Or, God forbid, Three).

Did that mean that True Love didn't exist in the first place or that it can come in an unexpected variation of numbers?

After returning to London with Hilal, Dunya's once passionate journey in pursuit of light turned into a desperate flight from it. She now sought shelter in darkness, which she found was a safe cloak under which she could hide—her heart.

Giving up on light also meant that Dunya had to abandon her camera, which she hid in the darkest cupboard she could find. In that same cupboard Dunya also hid all the photographs she had taken of Suha. She could not bear to throw them away, nor could she show them to anyone, especially not Hilal.

"All of Suha's photographs were overexposed," she told him. "There was too much light."

Dunya could no longer touch her camera because there was nothing she wanted to photograph now that Suha was gone. After taking those last few photographs of her, Dunya could not imagine taking any other photograph.

During her first night in London, Dunya Noor could not sleep. Instead, she went upstairs to the loft where Hilal kept his biggest telescope, with its large eye facing the dark night. She sat down on a stool and searched in a specialized book of stars to find out which direction she must point the telescope in order to be able to gaze in the direction of the constellation known as 'Mizar and Alcor.'

These were two stars, which always came as a pair, one of which is visible while the other invisible. To Dunya they were Hilal and Suha. Perhaps by contemplating this double star, she would find an answer to her new question: how can One True Love possibly be torn into Two? Can one describe such love as True Love, or does its division into two mean that it is no longer True, but False and invalid?

She looked up at the night sky through Hilal's telescope. She closed her eyes. *Where are you Suha? Where are you? When and how will I find you?*

In the silence of that night, and the many nights after it, Dunya could feel the broken parts of her heart, each one like a spark of light shooting up into the sky above her, each one calling out Suha's name.

Suha, Suha, Suha.

She gazed up into the sky, where she wished her secret love for Suha to hide—a truth she could never tell.

Hilal did not dare admit it to himself, and he wondered whether he was imagining things, but was Dunya Noor losing her light?

Ray by ray, sparkle by sparkle, hour by hour, and day by day?

He watched as Dunya appeared to be disappearing right in front of his eyes, piece by piece, curl by curl, minute by minute, night after night. It was as if she were melting away, dissolving like sugar. Why was this happening to her?

He had always known that Dunya was the kind of girl to whom the most unexpected things would happen, but he had never expected this: that she would leave him while still in plain sight.

That light would become dark and day turn into night.

After many months like this Hilal could not stand it any longer and he opened the cupboard where Dunya had hidden all the photographs she took in Syria, as well as her camera.

He picked up an entire stack of photographs and began to carefully examine them one by one. And there, as he had known all along, he found not one, nor two or three, but many photographs of Suha. But there was one photograph which caused him the most pain to look at. It was of Suha sitting on her bed with her bare arms spread out like wings—and light, an intense brilliant light, shone all around her. On the back of that photograph in Dunya's handwriting he read the following words: the last photograph.

Hilal held it in his hands like a document that proved everything. He could see it. He could see the truth and he understood it.

This photograph was a declaration of love.

That night, Hilal lay next to Dunya in their bed and could not sleep.

And before the next morning broke he began to cry. His tears fell silently one by one by one.

They fell next to Dunya.

Each one falling near to her but never on her.

Each one falling somewhere different.

Then in the end they circled her silently, One by One by One.

Not long after that, Hilal opened a small letter, which was waiting for him on his desk at the Moonology Institute in London, postmarked: Istanbul.

> I live above the Oud School in Istanbul. I want to see you, Brother. Come to me and bring with you Dunya. Without you and Dunya, my heart is empty. I cannot sing. Forgive me for running away, Suha.

And so Dunya and Hilal found Suha Habibi—a 'New Rising Star,' according to a poster they saw next to the local grocery store, on a stage in the Oud School in Istanbul—soon after she began making a name for herself in the city as a young woman who sang beautiful Arab songs and played the oud 'Like No One Else Could' (also according to the poster).

They came in during her morning rehearsals and heard the gentle words she sang into this large space and which filled the hall with their powerful reverberations. As Dunya and Hilal entered the large hall full of echoes and broken fragments of plaster and hundreds of pieces of stone that carried memories of ages long gone, these were the words that Suha sang:

Hold me or I'll fly.
Hold me in your eyes,
Hold me in your arms.
I am here because you can see me.
If you can't see me I disappear.

As Suha's beautiful voice rang through the hall, Hilal took a chair and used it as a ladder to help him reach his sister high upon the stage. He climbed up and ran toward her and tightly held her in his arms.

As Dunya looked at this sister and brother, she smiled to herself: they were two, the man and woman who lived in her heart, two who were now in each other's arms, *two broken parts reunited.*

Dunya looked on as Suha cried in her brother's arms and saw how she, in turn, dried his tears with the sleeve of her gold-trimmed dress.

The sister and brother's black wavy hair merged into one, their cheeks glued to one another, their hands holding each other tightly. There was silence in the hall. Silence, silence, beautiful silence.

She heard the silence in the room and saw how the morning sun came like a river from the sky and bathed both Hilal and Suha in its floods of light.

For the first time since Suha had gone, Dunya took her camera out of its case and directed her gaze on Hilal and Suha who now were looking at her.

It was summer, and what Dunya saw through her lens was *him* and *her* both looking at her: looking, looking, looking.

They were sitting next to one another on a blue corduroy sofa on the edge of the old dilapidated stage. Hilal in his blue jeans and a white shirt and Suha wearing a white gold-trimmed dress.

"Dunya," Suha called out.

"Come here, Dunya." Hilal said loudly. "Come and sit with us, sit here between us. You don't need your camera, come."

A bright light shone all through the room, sweeping away at every dark shadow.

Dunya looked at Suha and Hilal one more time through her eyepiece. She had to take this one last photograph: of Suha and Hilal who, through her lens, were becoming brighter and brighter. The light appeared to connect them in its large circle.

The light that connected them and that drew her to them became brighter and brighter still.

Dunya tried to find the right moment when she would press the shutter.

"Come, Dunya, come," she heard them say.

She pressed the shutter and then she ran, she ran toward Suha and Hilal.

Later, when that photograph was developed, no one who looked at it could see two people sitting on that blue sofa upon the wooden stage.

They all swore that it was just One.

Epilogue

THIS IS A COPY OF a framed letter which the manager of Café Taba, Mr. Hassoun, received one June afternoon, inside a parcel containing an old suit, a mustache, a fez, and a few other items of professional disguise. They were sent to him Express Delivery (postmarked Istanbul) by one of his all-time favorite hakawatis who was now (as he'd once predicted) a singer of great renown.

To Mr. Hassoun and to the Loyal Customers of the Great and Glorious Café Taba (Exclusively Reserved for Men),

That suit was a costume, my mustache was not real, my eyebrows weren't mine, nor my deep and booming voice. I leave them all behind. Never again will I hide my true self, nor fear the truth. I will throw away all disguises and dare to be real. And from now on my voice will be loud and clear for all the world to hear.

Yours faithfully
Suha Habibi (aka Nijm the Hakawati)

Glossary of Names

Most names in Arabic have a meaning.

Dunya: the world, fate, or destiny
Noor: light
Hilal: a crescent moon
Shihab: a comet
Nijm: a star
Suha: a star whose light is almost impossible to detect with
    human eyes, often used to test the sharpness of one's eye-
    sight. Also a word used to describe a state between waking
    and dreaming. In the Western constellations Mizar and
    Alcor or Horse and Rider, Suha is Rider or Alcor, and
    they are also part of the handle of the Big Dipper.
Suad: a happy woman
Said: a happy man
Basma: a smile
Bassam: the one who smiles
Farida: unique

Acknowledgments

I OWE A DEEP DEBT of gratitude to two talented and special women: Olympia Zographos, who has been a rock for me and a dear friend and editor, from the first few sparks of ideas that led to this novel until its last paragraph; and Nemonie Craven Roderick, my literary agent (Jonathan Clowes Ltd) whose insight and vision and faith and perseverance were key in more ways than I can describe or ever pay back.

Without the following people's support and inspiration and invaluable advice this book would not have made it to the finishing line: Rosie Welsh and Ann Evans (Jonathan Clowes Ltd), Ilonka Haddad, Kinda Haddad, Aboude Haddad, Tarek Hard, Issam Kourbaj, Ilona Karwinska, Hala Mouneimne, Ewan Fernie, Ulli Huber, Bego Garcia, Louise Carolin, Jessica Woollard, Katie Holland (Hoopoe Fiction), and Christine Garabedian.

And last but not least is my editor at Hoopoe Fiction, Nadine El-Hadi, who is the best editor I could have hoped for and whose sharp eyes and keen mind saw what I could never have seen on my own.

This book is dedicated to Syria and her children, both girls and boys, women and men, whose light will shine bright into the future and who will rise above all the suffering that is being heaped upon them. As the saying goes: "They tried to bury us, they did not know we were seeds."

I also dedicate this book to my father Marwan without whom I would not have had the fortune to also be a child of Syria, and whose love for his beautiful country was deep and unbreakable.

Although the historical and geographical settings of this novel are drawn from my own life in Syria as a child and teenager, the plot and main characters of this book are entirely fictional.

SELECTED HOOPOE TITLES

No Knives in the Kitchens of This City
by Khaled Khalifa, translated by Leri Price

The Baghdad Eucharist
by Sinan Antoon, translated by Maia Tabet

Of Sea and Sand
by Denyse Woods

*

hoopoe is an imprint for engaged, open-minded readers hungry for outstanding fiction that challenges headlines, re-imagines histories, and celebrates original storytelling. Through elegant paperback and digital editions, **hoopoe** champions bold, contemporary writers from across the Middle East alongside some of the finest, groundbreaking authors of earlier generations.

At hoopoefiction.com, curious and adventurous readers from around the world will find new writing, interviews, and criticism from our authors, translators, and editors.